DANCE MOVE

Also by Wendy Erskine

Sweet Home

DANCE MOVE

– Stories –

Wendy Erskine

PICADOR

First published 2022 by Picador
an imprint of Pan Macmillan
The Smithson, 6 Briset Street, London EC1M 5NR
EU representative: Macmillan Publishers Ireland Ltd, 1st Floor,
The Liffey Trust Centre, 117–126 Sheriff Street Upper,
Dublin 1, D01 YC43
Associated companies throughout the world
www.panmacmillan.com

ISBN 978-1-5290-7967-8

Earlier versions of some of these stories were originally published in the *Irish Times* and
in *The Stinging Fly*. 'His Mother' and 'Gloria and Max' were both broadcast on BBC
Radio 4. 'Secrets Bonita Beach Krystal Cancun' was published as part of the
Walking Wounded Series (Sick Fly Publications/Tangerine Press.)

1 3 5 7 9 8 6 4 2

A CIP catalogue record for this book is available from the British Library.

Printed and bound by CPI Group (UK) Ltd, Croydon, CR0 4YY

Visit **www.picador.com** to read more about all our books
and to buy them. You will also find features, author interviews and
news of any author events, and you can sign up for e-newsletters
so that you're always first to hear about our new releases.

Contents

Man was made for Joy & Woe
And when this we rightly know
Thro the World we safely go
Joy & Woe are woven fine
A Clothing for the soul divine

—from 'Auguries of Innocence'
by William Blake

DANCE MOVE

Mathematics

The drawer beside Roberta's bed contained remnants of other people's fun: a small mother-of-pearl box, inlaid with gold, a lipstick that was a stripe of fuchsia, a lucky charm in the shape of a dollar sign. Anything left behind in one of the hotels had to be put in a box and kept for two months. A girl who used to live in the house told her that. Didn't matter if it was a pair of tights or a phone charger, it was put away and then, at the end of that time, it was offered to the person who had cleaned the room where it had been found. That girl had got a little clock that way. But Mr Dalzell didn't operate like that. Mr Dalzell had said that anything she found was hers, automatically. Finders keepers, losers weepers. Except if she found a weapon. Any guns just pass them over to me, Roberta, he laughed.

Some things didn't make it to the drawer. Roberta would run her finger along traces of powder to see what would happen. The big flat that overlooked the river, the one with the ceiling to floor windows, was a fine spot for the powder. She often found tablets too. One lot she kept for the Saturday night when she was in her slippers and dressing gown. Her heart felt it was going to burst through her ribs. Occasionally she gave away the things she found, like the bottle of perfume that was worth over a hundred pounds. It smelled like the sawdust in a hamster's cage. Igor took it. He puffed it on when he was dressing up for a night out. The smell hung in the hallway. But most stuff needed to be bin-bagged: dirty knickers, grey bras, empty blister packs, bottles, blades.

One time the green-door house had syringes and burnt foil everywhere. That was sad because Roberta associated the place with families, like the people who left behind a game that she tried to play. She divided herself into two teams but even though she read them a couple of times, Roberta couldn't understand the instructions. The family left a small box of chocolates and a card on the table, saying thank you.

Roberta had encountered Mr Dalzell when the agency sent her to a restaurant for a three-day trial. The woman in charge there told her, and the other people entering the world of work, that it was important to turn up on time, dress sensibly and, most importantly, listen carefully to what they were told to do. They should take in every word and if necessary ask for clarification if they weren't sure. On the first morning, the chef gave her an apron and told her to wash her hands. He showed her how he wanted her to cut the vegetables. She looked attentively at the way he held the knife. You think you can do that, love? he said. He let her practise with a few carrots. Then he said, see this bag of peeled spuds here? I want you to cut them just the same way. We are making a thing called dauphinoise potato. She nodded. So, love, do you think you can do that?

It hadn't been easy to use the point of the knife to get the right small circular shape. When the chef came back he saw she had cut discs of potato the same size as the carrots. He smiled and said not to worry, that he hadn't explained it very well, and that she should maybe polish some knives and forks. At the end of the day, he got one of the guys to show her how to mop the floor and clean the place down. That was what she was doing when Mr Dalzell came into the restaurant to sit down at a table with the owner and the chef. Now there's a girl who knows how to work, Mr Dalzell said. She could hear the chef telling him about the potatoes. Followed instructions to the letter, he said. The total letter. Mr Dalzell surveyed the gleaming floor. How'd you like to come and work for me for a couple of weeks? he asked. But the couple of weeks had become over a year.

Mr Dalzell had provided her with training. A woman called Ava showed her how to clean the rooms, change the bedding and towels. She got to know when properties were rented by schoolkids for their parties by the pizza boxes and empty cans. She got used to the sick and even the shit. There was always the box of rubber gloves. She had got used to blood. There was one time when a laminate floor had been gluey with it. Stuck to the hall was a clump of black hair. Under the sofa she found a tooth, shreds of gum still attached. Mr Dalzell had been good to her. He owned the house where she lived. He sorted out the boys. They hung outside the shops, shouted at her, threw things. She shouted back. Listen to Crackers going crackers! they laughed. Mr Dalzell got to hear about it and then their eyes slid away from her when she walked by. One boy got a face all puffed with bruising.

Mr Dalzell got her a phone so that she could communicate with Gary Jameson. Every morning, she waited for him in the kitchen, which was always a mess. There were the plastic containers thick with the dregs of Igor's protein shakes, the dirty dishes in the sink, the spatter of hot sauce that the girl from Donegal made down the cupboard. But she was only going to tidy things up if she was being paid. When she got into Gary Jameson's van, he would always say the same thing: Another day, another dollar. He gave her a list of the day's jobs and she studied it. In the back of the van there were sheets, duvet covers, pillowcases and towels, their freshness almost aggressive.

Whoever wrote the schedule knew how long each place took to be cleaned. A little flat might only be an hour. Others, like the big three-storey place, took so much longer. Gary Jameson sometimes waited outside for her, but often he went away. There were other things he needed to do in the area. Later on, he would pick up the bags of laundry and rubbish. Gary Jameson had the keys for all of the houses on a big metal ring decorated with a cockerel. Each key had a tag with the number and street name of the house. He would take off one of the keys and give it to her so she could let herself into the next place. Don't lose it, he said. Don't. Fucking. Lose. It.

In her little book, Roberta had all the addresses written down and all the buses she might need to get, if she couldn't walk from one place to the next. It helped to put the details in the book, stopped them floating off. There'd come a time when the board at school almost looked underwater. The numbers flew out of her head, and words too. She would see them congregating in the corners of the ceiling and beg them to return to her head. They smirked, and said, nope. She started to divert her attention to the birds on the roof of the mobile classroom outside, and the tree that grew in the middle of the playground. It rustled. It looked so friendly. She didn't like going out to play at lunchtime. Since when had they got so complicated with all the rules? No, you don't throw it to her! We told you! You are not doing it right again! She said to him late one night, as she was going to bed, Daddy, I fell and hurt my head. It was a couple of months ago, I think. Well, that'll harden you not to do it again! he said.

On the Tuesday, the first place, a small flat, was spruced up within half an hour. The next one was more work because the people had stayed for a week; they had made it their home, with their toothbrushes still in the glass, the ring around the bath. There were clippings of nails on the floor. Roberta bagged up the dirty towels, put out the new ones. The third place was on the edge of the park. Ain't nothing like a house party, Gary Jameson said, as they drove there. Party house, this place, last night anyway. Give me a ring when you've finished, Roberta. He gave her the key and she got the bags from the van.

Although someone had opened a few of the windows, the house smelt of smoke. In the kitchen there was a pile of broken glass, pushed over to one of the corners. At the side of the sofa there was an old condom, the colour of frogspawn.

She went round with a bin bag, filling it with bottles and cans. It had been some party, for sure. The vacuum cleaner was in a cupboard under the stairs. It needed to be emptied and Roberta did this the way she had been shown. Always so much hair: a brown bird's nest of the stuff. After the hoovering, she polished the surfaces, then went upstairs. There was piss all over the bathroom floor and the towels were a ton weight because they were sodding wet. In the first bedroom there was another condom. She stripped the bed, which was streaked brown with fake tan, put on the fresh stuff.

The day she hit her head they had gone to the derelict place, the old Kane garage, Roberta, her sister and Desmond Kane. They were up on the roof and next thing she woke up with the sky a burning blue and Desmond Kane's face above her. He carried her home on his back and her sister put her in bed with a hot-water bottle. Don't tell where we were or what happened. Her sister brought up a bowl of soup but she couldn't drink it. It's the flu, her sister said. You have the flu.

When she opened the door of the smaller bedroom, a little girl—about eight or nine—was sitting on the floor. She looked up at Roberta, who stared at her and then closed the door again. People had been found in the houses before. A pair had once been still asleep in one of the beds. Gary Jameson got them out pretty quickly. Roberta remembered their frightened faces. She looked to see if Gary Jameson was still outside, but he had gone. She stood on the landing before opening the door again.

I've been waiting, the girl said. Waiting for my mum.

Roberta didn't reply.

Is my mum downstairs? she asked.

Roberta looked at the floor. No.

Oh, the child said.

She had a basic face, as if someone in a hurry had drawn quick features on a pebble. Her brown hair was in a thin ponytail. She wore pyjama bottoms and a school sweatshirt with a logo of three children dancing in a circle above the words Newton P.S.

Did your mum bring you here? Roberta asked.

Yes. And I stayed in the room like she said.

You were meant to contact the police if you found a child. But Roberta didn't think Mr Dalzell would appreciate her contacting the police. Plus, she had another job soon. Think! Think! Maybe she should contact Gary Jameson.

Am I leaving now? the girl asked.

The mother might have got stuck somewhere. Maybe the mother intended to come back. Maybe the mother had started feeling sick somewhere. She might have fallen in a K-hole. There was one time when the young guy who lived in the house was laid out in the kitchen after taking ketamine and Roberta thought he was dead. But a while later, he was back to normal. People might take the child away from the mother if they knew she had been left alone in a house like this.

Where do you live? Roberta asked.

We've only just moved to the new place. I don't know the address.

But that's your school, yeah? Roberta pointed to the sweatshirt.

The child looked down. That's where I go, she said.

Well, said Roberta. I wonder what we should do. I am going to have to make a plan. Okay, she said. I have got the plan. You are going to stay here and then I will come back for you. You'll know it's me because I will knock like this. Four times. Loud soft loud soft. And you will let me in.

Okay, the child said.

Roberta was waiting outside when Gary Jameson came. She loaded the black bin bags into the van and gave him the key. On the way to the next place, he stopped at the garage to get petrol. He ambled across the forecourt like a cowboy going into the saloon and expecting a shoot-out. Roberta's hands were shaking as she reached down to get the big key ring. Place with the yellow fob, place with the green door, big windows, the window-box one, where could they go, where could they go, not the park place and then, yes, do it, the gloomy old place that hadn't been used in ages, yes, thread the key off the metal before he is back. Gary Jameson was there with a bar of chocolate for her.

Thank you, she said. Do you want a piece?

You're okay, bird.

This next place, Roberta said. Just let me in and then go because I don't need a lift back home again. It's alright. I'll leave the bags round the back for you.

Oh, is that right now? he said.

Yeah.

You must have a boy on the go.

I might well, she said.

After, she headed back to the house where the child

was. She knew what she would do. She would take her to school the next day and by then the mother might be ready to pick her up. Or someone else. A granny or a sister. She would keep her safe until then. There was no need for the police.

Loud soft loud soft. She half-expected the child to have gone, but there she was.

Good girl, let's go, Roberta said.

The child was wearing a coat. But she was still dressed in pyjama bottoms, now tucked into boots.

Do you wear that to school?

No, the child said. I wear a school skirt and socks. But I don't have them with me.

Well, they would need to get those things. Roberta and the girl walked side by side when they left the house. Adult and child, Roberta said when they got on the bus, waiting for the bus-driver to query it, but he didn't. Adult and child, she whispered to herself, as they made their way down the aisle to a seat at the back.

In the town, they found a shop that sold school uniforms on the second floor. Roberta held up a couple of pleated skirts to the child.

You're skinny, she said. But I'm not. And now—she shoved the skirt down inside her coat—I'm even less skinny than I was before. You need socks too?

Yes, and the girl said she also needed a schoolbag. Roberta paid for that, a cheap one with a cat on the front. After walking around for a while, they sat down so that Roberta could copy in her little book the bus times and the route to the house and back again. The girl watched her, gave her a smile when she raised her head from the book. She told Roberta that the school started at nine o'clock.

When they got off the bus, there was a shop on the corner where they got cereal and milk. The girl said she didn't need a lunch for the next day because she got dinner in school. The hall was dark when they entered the house, but Roberta didn't know where the light was. When she eventually found it, they both looked down at the various letters on the mat, the numerous promotions leaflets and menus for takeaways.

Well, the postman left a lot of those this morning, Roberta said.

The living room had thick and dusty brocade curtains and a red velveteen three-piece suite. The carpet was big blowsy flowers ready to burst into bloom. The girl sat on the sofa with her legs tucked under her, staring up at the cobwebs where the walls met the ceiling.

Is it just you who lives here? she asked.

Yes. Just me. That's the way I like it.

Because it was so cold, Roberta looked around to find an old blow heater. It smelt of burnt plastic and kept cutting out, but it generated some sporadic warmth.

Today I don't really feel like cooking, Roberta said, so we'll just have cereal for tea. Okay?

Okay, the child said.

They sat by the heater, the occasional sound of the spoons clinking off the bowls. All of a rush the child said that the reason her mum brought her was because one of the times she was left before, she tried to make herself something to eat and she started a fire because the kitchen roll got caught on the flame. People had to come to put it out and her mum was very, very angry when she came back.

Roberta considered this. Things catch fire, she said. It wasn't your fault. Wasn't your mistake. Eat up.

People make mistakes, big fat Xs all over the work and that teacher always watching, even if you scowled back. They put her at a desk by herself where people from the past had gouged their names in the wood. She put her name along with them. Then they lifted her out to sit in the little room with the plant and box of tissues to speak to the woman in the cardigan who made her say numbers backwards, find words in a swirl of colour. Mistakes again, so they sent her to that other school with its buses, where she had to sit with a plastic bag on her lap because she was sick every journey. When she looked out the window, people made faces, did things with their hands. She slowly mouthed *Fuck you*, which surprised them.

What time do you go to bed? Roberta asked.

Half eight, the child said. But can I read for a while?

You can.

Does my mum know I'm here?

Don't you worry, Roberta said.

Later, Roberta prepared the room where the child would sleep. She shook the pillow, folded the corner of the duvet so it looked welcoming, wiped the chest of drawers and window sills with an apple disinfectant that she found under the sink.

The child was at the door. Will I go to bed now? she asked.

Yes, Roberta said. Take off that sweatshirt so it's good for the morning.

The child did that. She put her head down and crossed her bony arms across her chest. Roberta went outside the room, took off her own jumper, then her T-shirt, then her vest. She put the T-shirt back on and then handed the vest to the girl.

Thank you, she said, the vest still warm in her hand.

When she climbed into bed, the child lay on her back, staring at the ceiling.

The reading! She needed to read. Roberta suddenly realised. She bounded back up the stairs with the brochures that had been put through the door. The girl sat up to read a promotional leaflet about PVC windows and fascia.

Thank you, she said. That's great.

The dark pressed against the window and Roberta put on the heater again. Cognitive, cognitive, said the woman with the cardigan. Nothing to do with falling. But if she had had a mother she would have taken her to the hospital and then she would have gone to the school with the blue blazer just like her sister. When the people talked, they thought she couldn't hear them, but she did. Disgusting the way she went off with her fancy man, they said. What's a fancy man? she asked her sister.

But her sister was in Australia now. She once sent her a postcard with a wallaby on it. It was on the fridge in the house although somebody had drawn glasses on it. When school finished she went to the place where she put coffee in the polystyrene cups. Lines of them, twenty cups per row. And then after that the restaurant where she cut the potatoes. And then, Mr Dalzell.

In the morning, when Roberta came into the room, the girl had already made the bed and was sitting wearing the stiff new skirt over the pyjama bottoms.

Well, you can't wear those, Roberta said.

I've got no pants.

Take off the bottoms and come down for breakfast.

Cereal again?

Yes, cereal.

In the kitchen there was a blunt pair of scissors. Roberta hacked at the legs of the pyjama bottoms to fashion a pair of shorts.

There you go.

That was a good idea, the girl said.

I got lots of them, said Roberta.

The gates of the school were painted red and yellow stripes; there were posters covered in Perspex telling about safety in the playground. From a distance Roberta watched the other parents kissing the kids, checking things in their school bags. A woman swept a boy's hair smooth from where his parting was shaved in. She hadn't brushed the child's hair. At the top of the stairs, as the girl was about to enter the big doors, she turned round and waved. Roberta raised her hand.

Another bus and a walk through the park took Roberta back to her own house. When she got into the van, Gary said, Another day another dollar. What did you and your boy get up to? On second thoughts, don't tell me.

He gave her the schedule for the day with a cut and swollen hand. In the morning there were a couple of flats, but then later on it was the big house on the Antrim Road. On the bus, the child had said she thought she got out at half past two. There was too much to do in that house for her to be back on time.

Could we go to that big one a bit earlier? Her voice sounded like someone else's.

Christ, you're not wanting to head off again with this fella?

No, I have to go to the doctor's.

I can drop you at the doctor's. How long you going to be? There's another place to be sorted after that.

Not sure, Roberta said. Not sure how long the doctor will keep me. What happened to your hand?

It's nothing, he said. Should've seen the other guy.

The two flats were easy. In the first one, the lavender air-freshener sorted out the smell of smoke. The other one was as if someone had enjoyed cleaning it themselves. They had stripped the bedding and left it on the floor, placed the towels neatly on top of it. She was back in the van in no time. It smelt different today. She said so to Gary Jameson.

Well, bird, you do not miss a trick, he said. It was new laundry people who used a different powder. The old ones had done the job for Mr Dalzell for a while, Gary Jameson said, but nobody was indispensable. These others were cheaper.

The house on the Antrim Road she called the wedding cake because of the ceilings like icing. There were paintings on the wall of fields and farmyards. Once there was a religious group who stayed there for a week or so; they left a lot of leaflets about the power of prayer and used sanitary towels. The people staying this time did not seem to have been religious. There were some bongs made out of Lucozade bottles. There were loads of dirty dishes heaped up in the sink. She couldn't remember how the hot water worked in this place. She would have to boil lots of kettles. Maybe she shouldn't go to the school at all. The child could have told the teacher that she had been kidnapped by a strange woman. The police might be waiting for her at the school. Or she could go, but stand on the other side of the road, casual. There was only an inch of washing-up liquid left so she filled the bottle with water to eke it out.

Gary Jameson was late. She looked at her phone. Ten minutes late. She wasn't going to be there for the child and she hadn't even cleaned that house properly at all. Corners cut everywhere. Mr Dalzell would not be impressed.

The van swung round the corner.

Thought you were never coming, she said, as she got in.

Desperate to see lover boy.

I'm going to the doctor's, she said.

Where's the place again?

She said it was near the Iceland shop.

What they treating everybody with? Bags of fucking frozen peas? How long you going to be at the doctor's? There's still that other house.

I don't know. I'll have to see.

Check you all of sudden, he said.

*

She crossed over from the Iceland car park to the school with its cluster of buggies in the playground, its semicircle of parents. When the bell rang, kids filtered out, some jumping from the top step, some clutching things they had made out of paper. And then the child was standing beside her.

Hi, she said.

Roberta looked around to see if anyone was watching them.

Hi, she said back.

Are we going home now? the child asked.

Well, I thought, Roberta said, I thought we could try to find your flat. Because your mum might be there. Now, which way do you think?

They looked up the road to the hills, and down to the shipyard cranes. That way, the girl said. That way for definite.

There's flats, tower blocks, up there.

The girl shook her head. No. This way. She started talking about how a boy had got shouted at that day for lifting the giant snail from the tank and putting it on his desk.

Maybe the snail liked it, Roberta said.

Maybe it did, said the child.

They walked past butchers' shops and chemists, home bakeries and key-cutters. At one point the child indicated to turn down a particular street.

You sure? Roberta said. Doesn't look like flats down here.

It was a street of brick terraces.

I thought, the child said. But I can't really remember.

It was starting to rain.

What are we having for our tea? the child asked.

You know what, Roberta said, I was going to do something called dauphinoise potatoes which is meant to be very nice, but I think we are just going to get something from the shop.

The phone rang and it was Gary Jameson wondering where she was. She turned away from the child and said that she was still at the doctor's. No, she didn't know how much longer she would need to be. A police car went past, its siren sounding. Gary Jameson would hear that and know she was out in the street.

I'll do it first thing in the morning, she said. But he had already gone.

The house seemed warmer when they returned to sink into the plush fabrics while they waited for their pie to heat. Roberta found raffia placemats at the back of a drawer and so she laid the table for the two of them.

I've got homework tonight, the girl said. Can you help me with some of it?

Certainly, Roberta said. Important that you do your homework.

After tea, she got out a maths book and showed Roberta the page where she had to calculate angles.

I can do this one, and this one, but not that one.

Their faces were close as they peered at the page, biting their lips at the mathematical notation. The child turned to look at her. Do you know? she said.

Homework's for kids to do by themselves, said Roberta, turning away.

Oh, the child said softly.

*

That night the child read her English book in bed. When she went to sleep, Roberta sat on the landing outside the room, her back against the wall. The door was ajar and she could hear the easy breathing. There was the slight sound downstairs of the blow heater, some nonsense on the television, that old one with a big bulging back. She sighed. No dashing, running around, leaping on and off buses. There was no need to think about anything just at present because it would be hours before the morning light would come and she would not mind if it took twice as long in its arriving.

On the way to school in the morning, Roberta said, I hope you remembered to put that homework in your bag.

The girl tapped it. Of course, she said.

There were some of the same people on the bus: the woman with the jungle print scarf, the man who was already wearing his work ID around his neck, the guy with the studded leather jacket.

You'll be waiting for me today, the girl said. We won't go walking around again. You'll be waiting for me?

Of course, said Roberta. She tapped the girl's ponytail. She'd forgotten to brush it again. But tomorrow.

By the time she got back to her own house, Gary Jameson was already there.

Dirty stop out! he shouted. I know what you're up to.

When she got in, she took a look at the schedule. They were starting with the place she should have done yesterday, fine. But there was a gap between the next house and the one at twelve o'clock. That would give her time to get to the shops. And then she saw that she was meant to clean another place when she was meant to pick the child up from school again.

I can't do that one, she said.

Roberta, Gary Jameson replied. Roberta. You are just going to have to sweetheart, because, you cannot fucking pick and choose. You got a job to do. You want to piss off Mr Dalzell?

They had been playing cards in this house. She knew that from the way everything was drawn round the table as if it was a magnet. She cleared that, attacked the blood on the floor in the kitchen, dried to rust. She did not want to annoy Mr Dalzell, who had been so good to her. But even so, there was time for her to get to the shops between this house and the next.

Back on the second-floor uniform area, she lifted a five pack of kids' pants, a two pack of tights and a cosy looking nightie for the child. It was easy enough to go down the stairs rather than the escalator, hide the stuff under her coat. Next, she went to a bookshop, wandered about until she came to the section called Study Guides. She had seen her sister with these what seemed like a long time ago. There was a shelf for Mathematics—so many of the books—and Roberta picked one that, when she flicked through the pages, seemed to replicate the problems of the other night.

She called into another shop to get sweets for the girl. There was a queue and as she waited she cast her eyes over the magazines and newspapers, she noticed the pictures and the headlines. A footballer had hit his girlfriend. All the papers were talking about it. But then in the local paper it was different. A woman had been found strangled. Murder enquiry. She was pretty, with her hair curled like that and her smile. Roberta got the sweets and then headed towards the bus stop.

It wasn't until she was crossing the road that she realised. She stopped and a car nearly hit her. The man rolled down the window and shouted but she didn't hear because she was running back to the newsagents. She lifted a paper and walked out of the shop. Josephine Claire Muldrew, twenty-six years old. There was another photo of her inside, a little younger, holding a child, whose face had been pixelated out. All that was there were her thin arms, a halo of hair. Mother of one.

A rough hand caught Roberta on the shoulder.

Do you mind? Who do you think you are?

He took the paper from her.

I've had enough of people like you, he said.

She gave him the money that she had in her pockets, ten pence pieces, five pence pieces.

Cheek of you, he said.

It was the centre of town, just after midday, and people were staring at the woman shaking and crying, looking at a notebook as if it contained instructions for living. Maybe she was on drugs. There was something not right.

The phone rang.

Where are you, Gary Jameson asked. I've been waiting this past fifteen minutes.

Sorry.

When you getting here?

I don't know.

He would be tapping the steering wheel with those cut fingers.

Going to have to tell Mr Dalzell there's a key missing, he said. You know anything about that?

No, she said.

Okay, Roberta. And then he ended the call.

Back at the school, no one was on the climbing frames. Hard to believe it, one said. Did you ever speak to her? Yeah I asked her where she got her jacket from once. Wonder what happened. I heard what happened. Strangled. Poor wee child. Police were at the school earlier, for the wee girl. Did you see? I know what happened. She was at one of them dodgy parties and then went off with some stranger to another house, you know?

What'll happen to the child? Roberta asked.

They all turned to look at her. A woman in a blue coat shook her head. Sad isn't it? she said. No dad on the scene, don't know if there's any family, maybe they'll find a relative or else she will be put in care.

Oh, there's a relative alright because the wee girl has been at school the last couple of days, another one said.

The bell sounded and out came the kids, some in football strips. They shrieked, jumped in the air, swung their bags round and round. Look! a boy said, as he came to his mother in the semi-circle. He was holding a single green shoot in a yoghurt carton. Slowly, gradually, they moved off as their kids turned up. They left and Roberta stayed.

She leaned against the railing, looked at where the pointed black roof met a white sky. She called Gary Jameson back, but it went to his answerphone. Ready to work! she said in a high, shaking voice. She still had the things for the child. The maths guide. A teacher came out, surveyed the empty playground, then noticed a jacket left behind near the climbing frame. Roberta sat down on the ground and opened her notebook. They had not said goodbye because there was no need to. Schools had playgrounds. In the whole of the place there couldn't be more than one hundred primary schools.

Hey mister, she shouted to the teacher. Can I ask you, how many primary schools are there in Northern Ireland?

I don't know, she said. Eight hundred maybe? About that number. Can I help you?

She scored out one hundred. That was a lot more, eight hundred. But there were fifty-two weeks in the year, and at least a couple of years when she would still be at a school like this, wherever they sent her. The maths book would be out of date, maybe, by the time they found each other. But there were lots of them in that shop, shelves of them, for people of all ages.

Mrs Dallesandro

Bye-bye, Mrs Dallesandro!

Giving a brief wave through the window as she walks away, Mrs Dallesandro sees the shadowy shape of the receptionist behind the desk with its enormous vase of lilies, but also the reflection of her own newly blow-dried brown bob, the sheen sliding down its length as she turns her head. The owner stopped doing blow-dries years ago: they were the province of juniors. But he still does Mrs Dallesandro's.

Tonight is their twenty-third wedding anniversary. Awkward number, twenty-three. It didn't really warrant a trip somewhere, they would save that for twenty-five, but tonight they'll go to a restaurant. Bobby loves a bit of theatre, and so this particular place with its various flourishes—cloches, things being flambéed—is right up his street. He's almost childish that way.

They will have wine and they will toast everything: each other, the children, the twenty-three years. Although many of the Italians here came to the city last century from Casalattico in Lazio, Bobby always says that his ancestors arrived much earlier, that they were artisan craftsmen brought over to do the fine plasterwork in Saint Malachy's Church. Who knows if that's true? But when they bought the house on Malone, Bobby employed some very expensive restorative plasterers to work on the crumbling cornicing. Only what his forefathers would have expected, he said. And so, on occasion, he also toasts the ceiling.

Twenty-three years. She has a black dress to pick up from the dry cleaner's, and one of Bobby's good suits. The black satin, a miracle of construction with its intricate internal boning, fits her well. Mrs Dallesandro has no idea why anyone her age would want to look rustic if they could possibly help it. She has never favoured anything remotely peasant style.

The nail-bar next, and the technician soaks off the old colour. The technician, she can tell, is a little nervous. Her eyes keep darting to the buttery folds of Mrs Dallesandro's beautiful handbag before settling back again on her nails. Her mouth is a line of concentration. Another woman arrives and it's someone who used to have children at the same school as Mrs Dallesandro. She asks how the boys are doing.

Fine, says Mrs Dallesandro. At least, that's what they tell me! she adds, with a smile.

She says this confident in the fact that her broad, smiling, straightforward boys have no secret traumas or neuroses and are, therefore, in fact, fine. They are both studying law, one in first and the other in third year. That was inevitable, really. Knox Dallesandro is the most high-profile law firm in the city. It was set up by Bobby's father decades ago. There's even something people say as a kind of joke when they've done something wrong: better call Bobby Dallesandro! A character even said it on a TV drama set in Belfast once. Bobby loved that. Mrs Dallesandro taught French in a school for a while before she got married, until her first son came along. She remembered the fug of the staffroom and people eating out of plastic boxes. It hadn't been a wrench to leave it.

When no question about her own children is forthcoming, the woman says anyway that they are also fine. Michael is on placement and will be home soon. Mrs Dallesandro can't recall the name of the woman's daughter. She has the vague recollection that she was good at sport. Olivia, the woman says, has a boyfriend now. Mrs Dallesandro indicates a shade on the colour-wheel the technician shows her. That's nice, the woman says, although it would be too dark for me. Although ill at ease, the beautician is pretty. Mrs Dallesandro takes in her too heavily drawn eyebrows, the lipstick that has come off, leaving only an outline. She has a baby-face. Bobby, of course, has had other people over the years and they usually tend to be younger. Mrs Dallesandro wouldn't call them affairs or relationships, since that would elevate them to a status they didn't warrant. She has never once felt threatened by them, and in fact she has sometimes felt a little sorry for the people involved, who thought they were perhaps going to get rather more out of it all than merely Bobby's dick. Yet that was probably the sum total of it, bar a meal or two, a nice hotel room possibly, and of course, plenty of charm. That one girl came to their house for the Knox Dallesandro Christmas party. It's like something out of a magazine! she heard the guests say every year. Well, it always is magnificent, with the big fire blazing and the decorations and the enormous tree touching that elaborately corniced ceiling. Mrs Dallesandro saw a young woman, ill at ease in an incongruously low-cut top, looking at her.

Perhaps she thought that Bobby's wife just didn't understand him, whereas she, with her wealth of experience, did. Or she assumed that Bobby, so dynamic and attractive in his own way, was married to an unattractive frump. But then she saw the two of them laughing at some joke or another, took in the gleam of Mrs Dallesandro's tanned legs, her high cheekbones. Mrs Dallesandro was very gracious. When the girl drank too much and had to retreat to the bathroom, she knocked the door gently. She paid for her taxi home.

Bobby spends a fortune on that Christmas party. He's always generous. Surely we don't need wine that expensive for all of these people? she said.

Actually, we do, Jennifer, he replied. It's only once a year.

He bought himself something special to drink when they won a big case. And he bought himself something good when they lost a big case.

Whatever the outcome, she always said the same thing. Everyone's a loser in the end, Bobby. The house always wins.

No one gets out alive, Jennifer, he would reply. This

would usually be followed by an invitation to have a drink.

The colour works well; she likes it against the tan of her skin. She puts first one hand and then the other in the light machine. The other woman, Olivia's mother, is conversing easily with the person doing her nails. They are talking about holidays. It prompts Mrs Dallesandro's technician, while she is doing the second coat, in three precise strokes on each nail, to ask whether she has any holidays planned. Yes, Mrs Dallesandro says, for the summer. They will be going away for a couple of weeks returning to somewhere they have been before. It isn't straightforward to get to, but once there, it is heavenly. The technician says that she isn't going anywhere special. Her gran died and she is going to take her holiday to help her mum clear out the house and sort it so that they can sell it. It's a project, she says. It's away in the middle of nowhere, a place called Ballyanna.

Mrs Dallesandro says that she knows the area well and asks whereabouts it is, specifically, in Ballyanna.

She explains and Mrs Dallesandro nods. Those houses on the way out of the town, set back into the hill, that pot-holed and lonely road.

Good luck with the project, she says, when her nails are finally finished. She adds a good tip onto her payment. She has had her bank card on the table from the beginning so that she doesn't have to reach into her bag with the new polish.

Mrs Dallesandro should go straight to the dry-cleaners but in the car she takes a left turn that sends her in another direction. Everyone knows her on this road with its patisseries and boutiques, its florists. At one point Bobby had asked her if she would like a little shop herself. The wife of a friend of his had opened one on that road. Mrs Dallesandro knew where it was. It sold small and beautiful things.

You've such good taste, Bobby said. You would make a real good go of it.

Can you see me in a shop? she said. Honestly, Bobby, can you? I'd alienate all the customers with my rudeness.

Better stay the right side of the counter then, he laughed.

I think that's wise.

To get to where she wants to be, Mrs Dallesandro has to weave across the roads lined with houses where students live, and then along the river and the side of the park. The Victorian terracing becomes cramped and the brick dirty. There are vacant lots, metal fencing around waste ground with peeling for-sale signs. There's a carpet warehouse, rolled-up carpets outside leaning against the wall, grey rubber like severed trunks. Where she wants to go is in between two takeaways, a Chinese and a Turkish kebab house. She parks her car on the opposite side of the street, near the pharmacy. No one knows her around here and that's why she comes. It's not that Bobby would be furious if he knew, but she would rather just keep it her own business. Bobby and even the boys complained about it, after the scare last year. Everything of course turned out to be fine but the advice was clear. Sunbeds were absolutely not a sensible idea. She understands that, appreciates it, but she is only ever using them in total moderation. She simply likes the lift it gives her because she is naturally sallow and has the kind of skin that needs sun to give it a glow. And they don't live in a place where there is much sun. Spray tans just don't compare. And so she goes to one of the places on this road, where no one knows her. Really, as vices go, it is hardly in the worst category.

Across the window there is a huge decal of a reclining bronze beauty in a bikini. There is a table outside for smokers and a fibre optic light sits on it, patiently changing colour from magenta to yellow to violet. When Mrs Dallesandro enters, there is pounding dance music. She asks if she can have a half-hour session and the woman behind the counter says that is no problem. In the waiting area, there are sachets of lotion with names like Tantric and X-ta-C, but Mrs Dallesandro doesn't need them because she has come prepared with a small bottle in her bag. There's a stack of magazines and a cardboard display advertising a weight-loss drink. She is shown to a booth and the woman indicates the button to press to cause the metal shutter to ascend and descend. The bars of the bed begin to glow white.

Left on her own, Mrs Dallesandro presses the button so that the metal shutter closes over and she is alone in this hermetic little corner of the city. She takes off her clothes slowly and carefully, folds them, lays them on the floor. She gets the bottle from the bag and applies the oil in sweeping circles, first on her legs, her calves and thighs, then across her stomach and breasts. Her skin is still supple and firm. When she lies back on the plastic, Mrs

Dallesandro closes her eyes and imagines that she is on a beach somewhere with white sand and azure water. The dance music refuses to allow it and she is tethered to this place and its reception area. She thinks again of the place that she and Bobby went last year, where they stayed in a beach-house with its own jetty, but it dissolves quickly to be replaced by a street in a dreary country town, not so very far from some dead grandmother's house, due to be gutted. The shops there were all hybrid: the fishing-tackle place also sold concert tickets, and the chemists, handbags and suitcases. She had just turned eighteen and was working in a newsagents that also did a line in homeware. The town didn't really need two newsagents and there was another perfectly good one that most people went to. But still, they had enough business to give her a part-time job during her last few months at school.

It was mainly the father and the son. The mother appeared only infrequently. The father was hearty, overly so, trying to be liked in a town that knew the people in the other shop since they were in prams. The son, Stan, stayed mainly in the backroom, unpacking stock, bundling up papers for deliveries. But he also spent a lot of time reading books and, occasionally, the odd magazine. There was a tower of paperbacks with pages folded down. He had been terribly hurt as a kid, in what, a fire? A fire in a hotel? Have you seen him? people said. Poor guy. Although, it was in fact really only his face. Only his face, as if that was minimal. His face was a web of grafts. One eye looked as though it could not close. His lips were missing. But Stan's body was untouched, what could be seen of it—his hands, and sometimes, if it was warm, a jumper pushed up to the elbows, his arms were tanned and strong.

Sometimes she worked out in the back too. Between shifts, she might hang around, because it was easier to do that than go the long walk home. They talked, although he didn't like her to look at him. Stan could be very funny and she became attuned to what it meant when he tipped his head a certain way, or when he crossed his legs as he listened to her talking about what she was going to do with her life. It meant tell me more, I'm interested, but also: I don't quite believe you. She had ideas then about doing all sorts of things. They changed every week with the colour of her hair. She asked him if he had read *Les jeux sont faits* by Jean-Paul Sartre. No, he said. What's it about? She replied that she didn't know. They'd only been given it last Thursday. He would ask her sometimes what she did on Saturday night and she would tell him about a place he had never been to, a disco in the local hotel.

Mrs Dallesandro thinks of the pile of magazines sitting in the waiting area, that cardboard cut-out advert. The summer was drawing to a close and she would be gone to university in a few weeks. She knew that it was one of the only things that she would miss, the quiet chat in the back of the shop. One evening when the place was closed and they were cashing up, she found herself, quite surprisingly, putting her hand on his. It rested there, that hand with its approximation of a French manicure, done with Tippex. Although his face was turned away, she could see that he swallowed hard. She took her hand off his and started filling some of the little plastic bags that needed to be packed full of change. And then she thought, there's only a couple of weeks to go, why not? No one will ever know. Her hand went across to his again and then down to the zip of his jeans. She pulled it down, slipped in her hand, felt soft material, felt smooth skin, but then he said no, to stop it. Sorry, she said. Sorry.

Bundles of old newspapers were in the corner, stacked high. They moved towards there and although she thought that he would sit beside her, he didn't. Instead he pushed her gently so that she was lying back. She pulled off her trousers and then her pants. And he was on his knees. He passed her something. It was a magazine. It was only when she had the magazine in front of her face that he started. Even now she can remember what it felt like, lying there on those newspapers, his tongue, her legs opening a little wider. The magazine had a sleek model on the cover, glowing with health and cash. She closed her eyes to shut her out, so it was just Stan and her own warm, wet skin. His tongue was inside now, yeah? When she put down the magazine to look at him, he stopped, even though all she could see was his brown hair. So she raised the magazine again and looked at the model.

The other times it happened and there were more, maybe five or six, he always passed her a magazine. Some of the other times, she actually opened the pages. She looked at glossy adverts for perfume, for cars, at interviews with people in beautiful houses. That was a long time ago, in a dusty backroom of a shop in a town in County Antrim with her boy Stan on his knees. Even now though it is exciting and in the tanning booth she slips her hand inside her pants. She tries to remember the feel of the newspapers beneath her. She sighs and thinks of Stan, wetter than she ever is in her own bed.

When she came back that Christmas she heard from her mother that the people who ran the shop had sold up and moved on. Pity of them, her mother said. Hope they have a bit better luck somewhere else. She asked around but no one knew where they had gone. She felt a pain in her stomach for a month or so, and she wondered if it was love. But then, it diminished until it was nothing. Mrs Dallesandro slips into her things again. She will have a shower when she gets home, rinse off the oil. Bobby won't know where she's been. She never looks too tanned anyway. It's not that she wants to be the colour of teak; it's just a warmth to her skin that she likes. It only takes ten minutes for Mrs Dallesandro to get to the dry cleaner's. One dress and one suit, pristine and perfect in plastic bags. Bobby always gets her a special little gift on their anniversary. She wonders what it will be.

Golem

It actually takes the taxi only ten minutes to get there from the hotel. Kind of erotic, that driveway, with its crunch of gravel and soft curve. As Marty pays the driver, Rhonda watches two women walking past in sorbet summer dresses. When they get out of the car, Marty and Rhonda follow the women who are heading in the direction of the music, the soft and happy chatter.

Look at them! Rhonda says. You should've put something better on you than jeans and a T-shirt!

Doubt it matters, Marty replies. Hardly think I'm gonna be centre stage, Rhonda. Hardly think I'm gonna be the star of the show.

They pass between the side of the big house and the wall covered by creepers and azaleas, hydrangea and clematis to get to the garden. That is where the marquee is, its awning flapping just a little in the breeze. At the entrance, on a white table, there's a wicker basket for presents. Rhonda deposits the photo of the young Eloise and her. It's wrapped up in silver paper, so no one sees the two of them as kids, perched on the bonnet of a car, wearing deely boppers.

*

The garden was empty and the marquee only half-erected when Eloise first looked out this morning. Edgar was there already with the hose and the noise-reduction headphones. He bought them to use when cutting the lawn, but now he wears them for tasks involving only slight sound.

Don't you miss the birdsong, Eds? she asked.

Not really, he said.

Of course he missed it. He was striking a pose, just as he did when he listened to that plinkety-plonk music with the geometrical shapes on the front. But Edgar had done the lot today: the caterers, the marquee, the invitations. He'd booked the flight home for Mimi and he had asked Martin and Rhonda to come over. Mimi's hair was black now and it suited her, Eloise thought. She'd seen a photo. They could go for a lunch, the two of them. When the caterer's van arrived, Eloise noticed the name in calligraphic script on the side. It might be nice, winter sunlight, a velvet sofa, to sit and do calligraphy for an indeterminate time. Was it considered art? Probably not. Oh well. Then the hairdresser arrived. She asked Eloise if she wanted it sleek, like last time. Sleek was like an otter, a thing arching its gleaming body by a riverbank. Or maybe a stoat.

No, I think don't let's go with sleek. What else is there? Voluminous.

Then let's have that as our goal then. Voluminous.

A little volume was more forgiving anyway. She liked to make an effort. If she read a book, Eloise always looked first at the picture of the person on the back. If it was a woman who didn't look like she was making the effort, she knew she wouldn't enjoy the contents. (Of course some tried the reverse, tried to tone down good looks with functional clothing or a crude haircut, but they weren't fooling anyone.) But those other sorts, with their sad frizzy hair and watery eyes, they would consider her stupid. And they would be right. Not so long ago she met a woman who told her how, after doing a couple of exams at the local college, she was studying for a part-time degree. It all seemed very straightforward. The woman had ended up finding out lots to do with medieval people. In fact, they became a passion. She was very taken with something called the Carolingian Renaissance. It wasn't so difficult to imagine herself also being interested in the Carolingian Renaissance, or in fact another renaissance. It needn't be that one, particularly. When she told Eds that she wanted to do a course at the college, he bought her a very good pen as a present. But when she went, the man at the front spent aeons talking about the features of classic liberalism. It was all quite impenetrable. Eloise decided to shift to Art, where she made a clay model of a frog, filled a notebook with charcoal drawings and made a time-lapse film of raspberries rotting. The teacher came round one day and said that she needed to figure out what she wanted to say and what was important to her. The teacher lifted the photo of a drainpipe that Eloise had taken.

Is this important to you? she asked.

Not really. It's just a drainpipe.

But I want you to consider what's important to you. She added gently, What would that be?

I don't know, Eloise said. All sorts of things.

Like what?

I don't know.

It was only when she was driving home that she realised what her answer should have been. Mimi. Mimi, my daughter is important. Mimi. Mimi.

On the way to the airport, Marty had been saying that he still couldn't understand why they were staying in a hotel.

Because, Marty, Rhonda said, did Eloise and Edgar stay with us when they came over to Belfast? No, they didn't, and so staying with them on this trip was just never going to be on the cards.

But when they came over, we never asked them to stay with us.

Well of **course** we didn't! Where would they have slept? Could you **imagine** those two on an inflatable mattress on the living room floor? Hardly think so.

Okay, so even though they asked us to stay—because let's face it they have fucking rooms galore—we have to say no, because they didn't stay with us, even though we never asked them to.

Yeah you got it, she said.

Even though it is going to cost us the guts of three hundred quid.

Yeah you got it.

Money well spent then.

Rhonda affected a serenity. Know what, Marty, it's actually not going to cost us anything. Because it's costing me. I am paying for the hotel with my money. And because I am paying for the hotel with my money, why don't you just shoosh?

There was silence until they got to the short-stay car

park. Taking the bags from the boot, Marty said, I would have to point out, Rhonda, in all fairness, that it's not really your money anyway. It's Noreen's.

Was Noreen's. A solicitor, flakes round her mouth from eating a croissant or other pastry, had told her just how much she and Eloise had inherited when their mother died. It wasn't much.

My money now though, Marty. My money now.

As they progressed through security, Rhonda dreamed of Edgar. Her mother, incontinent, dazed, aching, had even so refused to go into a home. Put me there and you will kill me, she said. Is that what you want to do? So before and after work in the hospital, Rhonda tended to her. At the end of a shift, when they were as usual short-staffed, Rhonda just wanted to flop rather than start work anew at her mother's. The home-helps were useless. Don't expect me to light a fire! one of them said. All I can do is switch things on or off! Eloise sent care packages of hand-creams and candles with complex scents. One time she posted some chilled desserts.

Rhonda got to Noreen's one evening, found her lying covered in blood. She'd fallen and hit her cheek on the grate. It needed ten stitches through paper-thin skin. Rhonda phoned Eloise to tell her. Even though it was Edgar who answered, she provided full detail on how long they had had to wait at the hospital, how it was bound to happen again, how it was all practically impossible, how it was unfair that everything was left to her to do, how enough was enough was enough was enough.

But Rhonda, he interrupted to say, Eloise and I can

help. In fact, Eloise and I should help. We should be doing more.

He said he would give her a phone call the next day and he did, just as she was loading sodden sheets into the washing machine. He'd had a chat with Eloise and if Rhonda thought it best that her mother should have full-time care in her own home, then they could certainly fund it. He would leave the exact arrangements up to her but he wanted to give her his bank details. And so she started thinking about Edgar, a man who had only ever represented polite conversation, fucking her. It began when she woke at six o'clock in the morning, thinking that she needed to get to her mother's freezing house. She had to light the fire and get her up out of bed, washed and dressed. Then she remembered. No. No. The carer would already be there. The duvet seemed softer, warmer, and the world was a more benevolent place. It wasn't money though. Rhonda despised all that stuff where women went drippy over billionaires, submitting themselves to some guy's every whim because he had the dirty cash. Gimme a shout when there's a film about a woman throwing it all away for a guy on the minimum wage! Rhonda would say. She phoned Edgar to express her thanks. He listened so carefully to all she had to say that she found herself telling him about her day at work. So it wasn't just the money. It was understanding and, in fact, know what, understanding was actually really, really hot.

While the little overhead vent on the plane had been blowing air in her face, Rhonda had been lying on a beach somewhere with Edgar. He had just brought her a drink in a tall glass. He rearranged the beach umbrella, and the little breeze stopped. She reached up and twisted the black plastic. It was endlessly sunny with Edgar and sometimes they lived in a house she had seen in an interiors magazine that belonged to a professor at Stanford; a house in Palo Alto, all greenness and beautiful wood. So warm there too. There was always golden late afternoon light when they had sex.

Sorry, Marty said. I shouldn't have mentioned to you about your mum and the money.

It's alright, she said. Forget it. At the end of the day, you're right. It's her money.

At the party in the garden, Marty and Rhonda still stand at the entrance to the marquee. There is a string quartet in evening dress on the left and there are a couple of young women in white shirts and black trousers, carrying trays of drinks in long-stemmed glasses. There is a smell of cut grass. Everyone knows each other: their easy laughter confirms it. Marty and Rhonda feel a little awkward. Then Edgar appears. Wonderful to see you! he says. Terrific that you could come! He gives Rhonda a little kiss on the cheek. Marty! he says. Guess what? I got beers. Rhonda smiles at Edgar, then looks away. But then she looks back at him again. A woman comes over to say that someone needs a word with Edgar. I'll be right back, he says. Eloise is just over there! She'll be thrilled to see you!

The air-steward's cheery voice thanked them for travelling with the airline.

What time are we getting back tomorrow? Marty asked.

You know I have to be in work super early to let those plumbers in?

After the debacle in the previous job, he was keen to make no mistakes in the new one. He had allowed the boy Dino out to pick up one of the team from the garage where his car was in being serviced. That wasn't permitted, but still Dino was behaving well, he wasn't a bad lad. But Dino had picked up a girl he knew, crashed into a car, and put an old woman in hospital. Before doing that he and the girl had stopped off somewhere to have a burger. It was all in the papers. Young Offender Burger and Smash Bender. Marty had to resign.

Getting back at a reasonable time, she said.

You looking forward to seeing Eloise?

The last time either of them had seen Eloise was the day of Noreen's funeral. They all went for a meal in the hotel where they were staying. The restaurant was so like an opium den, it was a relief to get into the bright white of the toilets, refreshing to see the arc of yellow against the white. He stood there longer than he needed to, until someone else came in. Edgar ordered wine from the menu the waiter gave to him. When the bottles of white and red were brought to the table, Marty asked for a beer. Afterwards, Rhonda said how rude it was. You could have passed yourself, Marty. I mean, there was red and there was white.

Neither of which was what I wanted to drink, because that was a beer.

That wasn't it at all. You were acting the big man. Don't think you are all that, pal, that's what you were saying. I'm not having your wine. I'm having a beer.

Okay, let me tell you this a minute. You seem to operate in a world where everything seems to mean something else entirely. It's all code. I ordered a beer because I am an adult guy and I felt like having a fucking beer.

Yeah yeah, I believe you. Keep on telling them.

But she had got it wrong. He had no problem with Edgar, the radiator king. His family had made a fortune through central heating and good luck to them. Edgar, as that type of guy went, was fine. He enquired about Marty's work, asked what made it difficult. He remembered about the BMX riding.

Isn't that usually for little children? Eloise asked.

Yeah well, that's actually a pretty common misconception, Marty said.

I've never really seen adults do it. But I'm sure little children would enjoy it.

Eloise, said Rhonda. Marty was in quite a big competition over in England. If you had been at that, you would have seen plenty of adults because it was an adult competition. He can do all sorts of moves and tricks. They require a lot of control.

Did you win a trophy, Martin? she asked.

Yes, he said.

Well done.

No, it was Eloise that he didn't like and never had. Bottom line: she thought she was better than Rhonda. Any time Rhonda spoke she looked bored. And then, when she spoke, it was something entirely unrelated to what Rhonda had just said. She was self-centred. Postnatal depression, fair enough, no joke, but why did they have to hear of it endlessly when Rhonda couldn't get pregnant at all?

At Noreen's funeral, the two of them stood side by side, like one of those 'before' and 'after' shots, Rhonda being the two stone heavier 'before'. So what he did was, he beckoned Eloise over. He's standing near one of those droopy crematorium trees. She comes over, unbuttoning her black dress as she does so. Sometimes he fucks her over the tombstone (Sorry, Noreen!) and other times it's over the bonnet of a car because the car park for the relatives and other mourners is only yards away. She keeps begging him to hurry up, but he just takes his time. Takes his time. Nice and slow. Harder, harder, she says. But he keeps his own pace. She turns round. Do it on my face, Marty, she begs. I might, love. Or know what, I might not. Let's just see how it goes.

When he finishes—without doing it on her face—he walks back to where they're all standing, forlorn and in black. He goes over to Rhonda, gives her a hug and a kiss. Eloise looks over, furious, and he smiles slowly, happily.

Let's go over, Rhonda says. There she is. There's Eloise.

She is standing with a group, who are laughing at what is being said by a man with a booming voice. Eloise is poised and beautiful in a lemon dress.

Happy Birthday! Rhonda says as she gives her sister a kiss.

Yeah, many happy returns, Marty says. He gives her a hearty pat on the back.

I take it these are relations? says a smiling woman in a long dress with safari detailing.

My sister, Eloise laughs. And this is Martin, my brother in law. When did you arrive?

About five minutes ago, Marty says.

No, I mean, when did you arrive over?

The little string quartet begins a medley of Beatles songs. The viola player nods and smiles, seemingly acknowledging the whimsical nature of this.

The party guests would arrive at seven. Many had been invited but there were only a few that Edgar really cared to see: Marty, obviously, and Mimi. There had been a problem with the marquee but they would adjust the bill accordingly. It was meant to have had a laminate floor and white sofas. It was a glorified beige tent, open along one side. Others had arrived with bundles of lilies in zinc buckets and piles of linen. Eloise, Edgar thought, might not appreciate the beige. They had recently had a room in the house painted white. Surely white was white, but Eloise had got charts of various whites because some, he was informed, were cheap. She knew about colour. A while ago she had painted a picture. He found it a little naïve but it had been chosen for an exhibition in the library. On arrival, they found a dot beside it because someone had bought it, so he feigned mild outrage that it was going to be in someone else's possession.

He was on the way to pick Mimi up from the airport. This he would enjoy doing because he liked driving. It wasn't velocity. He didn't care about going fast. He would happily go on an endless journey, driving in silent darkness on smooth, unspooling motorways. He didn't even especially care for cars per se, even though he got a new one every two years. He always used the same dealership; they sent him invitations for new views and promotional events. He went once. They showed a video of a new sports car on a massive screen and people passed round trays of miniature burgers. But Darren wasn't even there. Edgar looked about the room, the shining chrome, gleaming paint, the crumpled looking individuals. He always got Darren every time he went. Darren was maybe in his thirties. He wasn't a typical car salesman: not slick or loquacious. He had no patter. In fact, he said virtually nothing, but filled out the paperwork with a world-weary air, as though it was sad that this beautiful and expensive new car would change precisely nothing. He didn't call him Edgar or Mr Bryans. He didn't call him anything at all.

Edgar had only ever seen him once outside that place. Eloise had a dreadful headache and they had no tablets so he said he would drive to the shops to get some. He didn't know why but he drove past the garage with its little shelf of painkillers behind the counter, and headed to the supermarket instead. Maybe it was because of the longer drive along an empty road lined by dark trees. He ambled around the shop because he wasn't sure where the tablets were. In front of a chilled cabinet, with his back to him, he saw Darren. He stood there compact and still. He was holding a basket. It looked sad, the basket. Why couldn't he just carry what he needed? Darren put a pizza in the basket which already had a carton of orange and a loaf of bread. Darren looked tired as he moved on, but perhaps everyone looked tired under the white lights of the supermarket. Edgar was there the next week, at the same time. He told Eloise they needed milk. He poured the last two inches of the carton down the sink. But Darren wasn't there, even though Edgar was systematic in his exploration of the aisles.

He wondered how Marty and Eloise's sister were getting to the party. Had he been told to pick them up too? He couldn't remember. He would need to check again with Eloise.

By the time they got off the plane, the shuttle bus to take them to the terminal was already full so Marty and Rhonda had to wait, with a handful of others, for its return. They were last off because Marty had got everyone's luggage down from the overhead lockers. Come on, Marty, wise up, Rhonda said. No need to act like Sir Galahad for every woman on the goddamn flight.

Marty wondered if the party was going to be wall-to-wall with ex-models. Eloise used to be a model. Noreen had loved going on about it, right from the very first night he had ever gone round to the house. So you know Rhonda, but have you met my other daughter, Eloise, the model? she'd said. Marty had once gone out with a girl who did the same sort of stuff, so-called modelling—in other words, handing out crackers with cheese at a milk marketing board event, or handing round plates of chicken drumsticks in a hotel in the town, while wearing shorts and a T-shirt. He mentioned as much to Noreen.

It's called promotions work, Noreen had said. And not everyone can do it. She's also been on the cover of a magazine.

What's it called? he asked.

Never heard of it, he said, when she mentioned the name.

You think any of those model friends of Eloise's will be there? he asked Rhonda, as they headed towards the car-hire desk.

Doubt it. Sure it was years ago. Doubt anyone would've kept in touch.

Funny how you are one of the best-looking people in your town but you head off to the big bad city and you're two a penny. You know, the teen queen hits Hollywood and she's washing dishes.

Well somebody has to get a lucky break.

Didn't happen for your sister.

Well, Rhonda considered. She met Edgar.

Don't know if Edgar is my idea of a lucky break. Right, let's get this car sorted out.

The man said that they could have an upgrade if they wanted, to an E-class Mercedes. It wouldn't be too much extra.

Why bother? Rhonda said. It's hardly any distance to the hotel. And there's no point getting a fancy car just to impress them because we'll be getting a taxi there.

Jeez, it's nothing to do with them. I just want to drive a different car. Yeah, that's what we are going to do mate, he said. Let's go for that E-class.

When Mimi appeared in arrivals, Edgar, as he hugged her, managed to kiss her enormous gold headphones rather than her cheek. Wow, he said. Those are impressive. But she explained that actually they weren't and that anyone who knew anything about them would know they were a piece of shit. She launched into a labyrinthine tale about various people borrowing and losing headphones.

He laughed. Okay, then, those are very unimpressive and shit headphones.

Her hair was black but there was an inch of fair at the roots. Her grey tracksuit bottoms were bulky but her skimpy white halter top showed her nipples. As they went towards the exit, he saw people stare at his daughter, at her white top. She wasn't as bad as he had seen her on some occasions, but still her shoulder bones protruded, her chest was knuckled. It was so long ago when it started, fourteen years of age, with that boyfriend who took the dreadful photos of her and sent them round for all to see. The police couldn't do much. But then it could also have been the school. Too much pressure. They sent her to another place. Too little structure. When they went all those times to see that fancy doctor who played Joni Mitchell in the beautiful waiting room, it was always her and him. Not Mum, she said. No way do I want Mum there. The journeys back, both of them faking a brightness that something was getting a little better.

You must be cold, darling, he said, when they walked to the car. Perhaps you should put on a jacket. Do you have one?

She said that she would only be staying for one night before she headed off to see some friends.

I'd love you to stay longer, he said.

Maybe I'll hang around another day. But only to please you, you crazy old fool. Who wants me to wear a coat.

She punched his arm, laughed, gave him a kiss.

Rhonda looks out from where she stands in the marquee to the beautiful big house and its garden. There is a patio area with fat tubs of flowers. The place is just looking so well, Eloise, she says.

Eloise has such a special sense of style, one of the women agrees.

I mean, it's so lovely, but can you remember, Rhonda says, when we used to play in that old back yard? We would do that thing, can you remember, when we were kids, where you put a tennis ball inside a pair of old tights and then you stood with your back to the wall and bounced it from side to side?

Sounds quality, Marty says. Anyone fancy giving it a go now? You got that big wall over there.

Mimi used to have tennis lessons from a young man who went on to be a reality TV star.

And do you remember, Rhonda says, that there was this other thing we did with elastic bands?

I didn't watch it but I heard that he was quite popular.

Don't really know, Marty says. There were a couple of girls who were pro-surfers. And there's always loads of fitness instructors isn't there?

Don't talk to me about fitness instructors! says the woman who thinks Eloise so stylish. She holds up her hand. Just don't talk to me about them!

Rhonda wondered about the party as she stared at the fields out of the window of the car. Hopefully it would just be Edgar and her, for at least some of the time. She wanted to tell him about her life, because he would understand it. So many things didn't compute, but if she told them to Edgar, they might become clear. When she came off the phone to him that time it was as if all had been rinsed in cold water. It's Edgar's house and she's drinking brandy in a beautiful glass, clinking the ice when she pauses in telling Edgar whatever she's telling Edgar. She's watching herself on a big cinema screen, her back arching, her mouth open. A physical manifestation of Edgar never really appears in her mind. He's just more of a presence, but what is annoying is how there's always a radiator in shot. It always sneaks in, the radiator. The only place it didn't appear was the beach.

So Marty didn't think that Eloise had lucked out when she met Edgar. Well, what did he know? Left to her own devices, things hadn't gone too well. Horrible to remember it, but things had not gone too well at all. The other times she came home from London she was desperate to go out with that crowd of hairdressers she knew, but this time she went straight to her room. She was thin anyway; it was like hugging a cat. Rhonda had always seemed to have an extra layer of muscle. This time, when they picked Eloise up at the airport, she was haggard. Back at the house she changed into a geisha-style dressing gown and took to her room. She was in there for the next two days, only emerging to make herself a cup of tea or to have a shower. You okay, pet? Noreen asked every time she appeared. You okay, pet? What's up? Rhonda said. Why don't you tell us what's up?

On the third day, Rhonda went in, opened the curtains and said, We are fed up with you moping about.

She said that she wanted to be left alone, told her to go away.

Rhonda sat down on the bed.

So—what's wrong? You better tell me.

I was—

And she put the arm of geisha satin across her face.

You were what, Eloise?

I got… hurt, she whispered.

Hurt? What do you mean? Who hurt you? What do you mean hurt, you mean you're upset?

She shook her head.

Then what do you mean?

Assaulted. She silently mouthed it.

Oh Eloise, she said.

Sexually assaulted. Again, mouthing the words.

Who by?

She was doing a shoot for a magazine. And after he said to her if she would like to go for a drink. Why not, she thought, but as they made their way down a flight of stairs, he pushed her against a wall, started kissing her, stuck his hand between her legs.

And then what?

He put his fingers inside me.

What a sleaze. What a perv.

Yeah, she sniffed. I know.

I'm so sorry, Eloise. But go on.

Go on what?

What happened next?

Well, there was someone at the bottom of the steps. There was an office below. He heard somebody coming, so he stopped, and I went off.

Lucky escape!

It was horrible. It was disgusting. She pulled the duvet up to her chest.

I'm sorry, Rhonda said.

It was the worst thing that has ever happened to me.

Rhonda said nothing.

The worst thing that has ever happened, Eloise said.

Noreen was shouting, saying that the tea was on the table.

Seriously?

Eloise looked surprised. Seriously!

Well, Rhonda said. It happens. Fellas are pigs. You know, I was only in fourth year when that happened to me. The guy's hand was like an iron bar. And it happened when I had that summer job in the hotel bar.

It hadn't happened to me before, Eloise said.

In a way, you know, I'm surprised about that. If I'm honest. Stuff like that, it's horrible and shouldn't happen, but it does—to plenty of people. And worse. Thing is, that world—modelling, photography, films, telly—it's seedy in its own way. You can dress it up with awards and all that, but some actress is getting paid to pretend to have sex with some grotty wee guy. What did Marilyn Monroe say when she got her first big contract? That's the last cock I'm going to have to suck. That's that world for you. So even though there's all the glitz and glamour you kind of know what you are getting into.

Eloise said nothing.

And so I suppose, Rhonda said, that that means I probably feel more sorry for some seventeen-year-old getting fingered round the back of the supermarket by the deputy manager, you know?

Eloise said nothing.

That's not to say I don't feel what happened to you was bad. But no need to take it personally.

Eloise didn't ever tell Noreen. She packed up her bags and went back to London the next day. And then a few months later, news came that she was now working part-time in an estate agent's. They had used her in their latest brochure; the picture was of her smiling and handing over an improbably large key to a smiling man in a suit. It wasn't Edgar, but Edgar did turn up, some months later, to sell a flat.

So yes, Edgar had come to the rescue. Maybe there would be a crackling open fire at the party, with the wind howling outside. It didn't matter that it was summer. Rhonda crossed and then uncrossed her legs. She just felt so hot.

Those heated seats in the E-Class, huh? Marty said. Pretty good.

Look, there's the sign for the hotel, Rhonda said.

Two people in the group drift off to speak to someone new who has just arrived and is waving over frantically. Another man joins the gang and starts talking to Eloise. He tells Rhonda and Marty that he lives just down the lane.

Is that so? Marty says. Sorry, excuse me a minute. And he heads out of the marquee into the garden where it's less stuffy. He takes a drink from one of the passing trays and sits down on a garden seat near the patio. He sees a girl leaning against a tree, looking at her phone.

Hiya, he says.

She carries on staring at the screen.

Did you hear me? I said hiya.

She looks up and says, Yeah, I heard you.

Not your kind of party?

What do you think?

Come on over here till I have a talk with you, he says.

She makes a pantomime of reluctance, but still she comes over and sits beside him.

I'm Marty, he says. And you're Mimi, yeah?

She gives him a smile of a kind that he has seen many times over the years. From girls, but boys too, fifteen, sixteen, seventeen, trying to be seen as worth something in the only way they know, by being a hot ticket. And she is still doing it at what age, twenty? He looks at her evenly, the way he does with the kids at work.

What do you normally do with yourself? he says.

I don't know. Not much.

Like what?

I don't know. This and that. Why, what do you do that's so significant?

Rhonda sees them talking from where she stands inside the marquee. The circle widens as a few more people join the group. Edgar is one of them. She can't look at him. Instead she looks at the ground. He is wearing little slip ons with the kind of rubberised soles that extend up the back of the shoe. They are for old people. All ideas of Edgar are eviscerated: Palo Alto, the beach, the fire. Vaporised.

*

Marty and Rhonda saw that the hotel had some half-hearted topiary. An old red dog lolloped down the steps of a shabby white building.

Bit of a dunderin inn, Marty said.

Shut up, it's a four star.

There was a huge white bed with a padded headboard. The bath was a sunken marble affair in the shape of a shell. Rhonda got out the dress she'd brought to wear, and the present for Eloise.

What is it? he asks.

A photo of the two of us when we were younger. It's in a beautiful frame.

I'll put on that other T-shirt in a minute, he said, continuing to lie on the bed.

We're both wearing deely boppers. Remember them. Those glitter balls on wire that you wore on your head?

Yeah. They were stupid.

The dress when she put it on didn't really suit her. It wasn't all about looks, but there was no need for her to wear stuff his granny would have worn. That dress, it was like a dressing gown, tied in the middle. Eloise would take one look at her and think aren't you just so fucking unimpressive.

That the only thing you got with you? he asked.

Why, what's wrong with it?

Just kinda, well nothing really, it's fine. Just wondered if it was the only thing you'd brought.

She undid and did the belt as though that would effect a transformation.

Oh yeah, that's better, he said.

Eloise, he imagines, is wearing those deely boppers and they are bouncing up and down, springing on their wires as he fucks her again. She puts her hand up to rearrange them, but he says, Never mind them. She's over the tombstone. She's over that car bonnet again.

Are you just wearing that T-shirt?

Yeah, why not?

You not making more effort?

Not really, no.

Well, you need to be on your best behaviour with Edgar. I would really appreciate it if you made the effort with him.

Make the effort to do what?

To be friendly.

I am friendly with him.

How long will it take us to get there?

Fifteen minutes tops.

The string quartet is playing a waltz. The girls have brought out square plates of food, decorated with nasturtium flowers. An old lady, another neighbour, is talking about how she used to have a huge number of nasturtiums in her garden. From a distance it looked like the house was on fire. Mimi is bringing a bike out of the garage. It had been there since she was a kid. It's greyed with dust, cobwebs on the handlebars.

Nice antique you got there, Marty says.

He wheels it across the lawn.

But can you still show me how to do a trick?

He rides around in small circles.

What's your balance like? Can you do this?

He stands up, his feet on the pedals.

The old lady is watching, thinking of her husband, long dead, who rode a bike every day to work. She remembers how the bottoms of his trousers sometimes had streaks of oil from the chain.

I probably can't do that, Mimi says.

Try it.

She can keep it poised for a second or two before it skews to the side.

Marty takes it back again.

Okay so, he says, what you need to do is sort your foot placement. You need to get that right.

Again he goes round in small circles, getting comfortable. Marty has been riding bikes since he was a kid, outside shops, in garage forecourts, under motorway flyovers. He lifts the weight of the bike off the ground. He circles, and then does this again, the bike moving off the ground a little more.

Edgar is looking over now, at this sight in his own garden. Marty is in a white T-shirt, his arms creamy and muscled. He thinks of the showroom, the new cars, the supermarket when it is late. Marty lifts the bike so that it hops with the front half off the ground. Edgar smiles sadly.

The bike hops again, first the front and then the back.

It's just not the right type of bike, Marty says to Mimi, laughing.

More people now, drinks in hand, are watching the spectacle.

Mimi, he says, bring over one of those there chairs would you?

She fetches a small white garden chair from the patio. He is able to jump over it. A couple of people clap.

Hey! Mimi says.

Eloise sees it, smiles in delight. Bikes! Now wouldn't that be a lovely thing. She and Mimi could go for a bike ride somewhere. They could hire them and it could be a pretty spot, dappled light, whizzing through a nice forest. But look at Martin and how he just seems to get on so easily with Mimi. How can he do that? How can you do that? Does he know what to say? She imagines going through the forest on her own, slowly.

Come on, give it a go.

Marty gets off the bike and hands it to Mimi. Try even just standing again, he says.

This time she is able to hold it for a few seconds. People, including Rhonda, continue to watch from the marquee. They look like a father and daughter. He would have been a good dad. She would have been a good mother. She thinks so, at least.

Marty takes the bike back again and once more hops over the white garden chair. They all clap once more. A few shout, Well done! And then the string quartet starts playing a sprightly version of Happy Birthday. The bike is left lying on the grass.

His Mother

In her bag, Sonya has a paint scraper, a cloth and a big bottle of soapy water. She has tried to work methodically, moving in succession along each of the radial routes coming out of the town. It's been a laborious process. She looks for green electric boxes and lampposts, the black street bins, but it could just as easily be gable walls, or even corrugated iron, the shutters of shops that have been empty for six months or so. She looks for anywhere where she can still see her son.

They had not agreed on the photo for the poster. Jade, Curtis's girlfriend, hadn't liked the passport picture Sonya wanted to use. It looks nothing like him! she said. Nobody'll recognise him! Jade wanted a photo of Curtis on holiday, where he was sitting outside a bar, a bottle of beer in his hand. Sonya asked Logan what he thought. He was studying the ordnance survey maps that he'd been given of forest areas in the locality.

Logan, Sonya said. Logan, did you hear what I said?

As long as you can see him clearly, does it matter which photo? Let's just get those posters out there. That was his answer.

By the time Sonya had got the pages photocopied in work, you could hardly see that fair hair that he got cut every three weeks without fail. A falling shadow made him look like he had the dregs of a black eye, when he'd never been in a fight in his entire life. It was his old football club that put the posters up the length and breadth of the city. They'd got in contact. Teenagers putting the posters up on electric boxes and lampposts even though they'd never heard of Curtis Rea. But she's cursed them sometimes over the last few months, cursed their commitment to the task.

Some put them up with Sellotape. Those ones have now long gone. The tape turned brown and then loosened. But the posters stuck with wallpaper paste have remained for much longer; they have taken the splatters from dirty puddles, got bleached by the sun. Posters that asked 'Have You Seen Curtis Rea?' ended up next to adverts for a tae kwon do club, a splashy flyer for a Back to the 60s night, a handwritten note about a missing cat called Boogie.

Curtis went out before his tea but didn't come back.

He'll be round Jade's. Round a mate's, Logan said. There was no need to be concerned.

Well, if you think so, Logan, Sonya said. I wouldn't want to make a fuss. It's not like him though.

In the morning he still wasn't there. They were sheepish calling the police, expecting to be dismissed as timewasters. By the end of the day, however, the police had found Curtis's car, his Corsa, left in a hotel car park near Shaw's Bridge.

Things happened to people. There was always that. They fell and hit their heads on pavements. Didn't even remember their own names. Ran into friends, ended up at crazy house parties, went off the radar.

The policewoman nodded when Sonya said these things.

What was his mood when he left the house? she asked.

Fine, she said. Tell you what, see those oven chips? Sonya remembered him saying as she was putting them on the tray. Make sure you don't take them out too early, give them a decent blast. Them ones are rotten when they're soft.

Enough of that or you'll be the one getting a blast, she said.

I'm only saying. They're rotten when they're soft. Gonna love you and leave you here for a min. Just nipping out.

But your tea is going to be ready soon!

Just nipping out.

Sonya sees the remnants of a poster on a lamppost. It's there just above the steel cable tie. She soaks the cloth with water from the bottle, then presses it to each of the corners, before moving to the rest of the poster. The cloth needs to be saturated for it to be effective. Sometimes the scraper lifts paint as well. The metal of the lamppost is surprisingly soft and she'll leave it scored and tracked. Sonya flakes off the faint digits of her own mobile phone number, the old one anyway. It had to be changed because of the number of calls she got. Well-wishers, but also kids. Hey missus, I think I seen Curtis Rea. He was having a pizza at the Ice Bowl. Hey missus, how much do you charge for a blowjob? On this lamppost, there is a religious sticker. It bears a Bible verse and a rainbow. In the weeks after Curtis, people from a church visited. Logan went along to a few meetings.

You could come, Sonya, he said. You get coffee. There's no sermons.

Not interested, she replied.

More recently he has started going to an evening class in A-Level Psychology. The fat textbook is always sitting on the sofa. At the beginning it was all, Listen to this, Sonya. He'd read something out as though it was a discovery. Do you think, you know, do you think, that that might have been something to do with it? Neurons was a word he used a lot.

I really don't know, she said. Because they really didn't know.

There were two weeks of coordinated searching of forest areas. So many people helped. Logan went, but not Sonya. Craig wanted to, but he was too young. He was angry when they said he couldn't and shut himself up in his room. Logan came back, his big hands torn with briars. Cold nights with the wind howling up the old chimney breast and Curtis was out there somewhere. When he was young, he always wanted the hall light kept on when he went to bed.

There came that afternoon when she broke off from cleaning the kitchen to see that she had six missed calls from Logan. Sonya knew that was it. She knew what that meant. But she couldn't bear to speak to him yet. When she heard the car in the driveway she began shaking so violently that she couldn't utter a word. When Logan came in he said, We've got him, Sonya, we've got him. And then he sat down on the bottom stair and started making a noise like a small animal.

They put Curtis in his good clothes for the funeral. Sonya took forty minutes to press his shirt, cleaned the expensive white trainers with the tiny silver lettering that were clean anyway. It was a sunny day at Roselawn. Logan stumbled his way to the end of a bible reading and Jade read some poem, breaking down halfway through. It was decided that the last song as people were filing out should be one that Curtis liked. Craig picked something.

Is it his favourite? Sonya asked.

Dunno, Ma. We didn't sit around making lists of our favourite tunes, you know? just know he liked it.

It was called 'Your Love' by Frankie Knuckles. It was pleasant enough at the beginning. But then a guy started sighing, huffing and puffing in a sexual way. Sonya didn't feel it was suitable for a funeral. But nobody seemed to notice, or if they did, they didn't say anything. Craig managed to get a paper cut from the edge of one of the programmes they handed out and got blood on the cuff of his shirt. After Roselawn they went to a golf club. Sonya busied herself helping with the food, which was chicken curry or beef bourguignon. Nearly everyone took the chicken. She couldn't stand it when Curtis's friends hugged her, the softness of their necks, the smell of their aftershave.

Sonya passes a bin but she doesn't see Curtis, only a poster for a long-past demo at the City Hall against pay cuts. Further along then, there's an electric box. A noise comes from these boxes, a hum like a pylon. When she moves away she imagines she can still hear it, the air quivering with the painful, insistent sound. Those placid people at the bus stop, can't they hear? Two young men walk by, laughing at something, and Sonya's watching hard. It seems like they're laughing, certainly, but the one on the left, is he really? She's done those oven chips over and over again and they are just right every single time now, just right.

It was a month after the funeral. On Sundays they always sat in the good room with the papers. The fire was lit and Logan had dozed off after lunch, the colour supplement across his chest. Logan didn't sleep at night either; she felt him twisting, getting up for glasses of water, checking his phone. As usual, Craig was upstairs. The clock on the mantelpiece said three o'clock. Beside it was their wedding photo and that orchid the people at work had given her as a birthday present. And then, propped up against the orchid, was the picture of the four of them in a restaurant in the town. At the end of the mantelpiece the old school photo of the boys sat, Curtis with his arm round the four-year-old Craig. Curtis's new teeth with the jagged edges were just coming through. His tie wasn't straight and the collar was pulled to one side. Could those dopey teachers not have tidied you up a bit before they let the man take the picture? she had said. In a rush it came to her that it was raining outside, and Curtis was out there, dispersed all over the city on the posters, the rain coming down on him. She grabbed a knife from the drawer in the kitchen and got into the car, Logan still asleep in front of the fire.

The Ormeau Road was one of the places that she knew they'd put posters. She remembered them saying, we did the whole length of the Ormeau. The first poster she saw was on a metal shutter. It's okay, son, she said, as she started scraping with the knife. It came off in long strips that time because even though she didn't have any water, the paper was soaked with the rain. But there were so many! She could see another poster across the road on the bus shelter outside the Indian takeaway, and another one further down on a lamppost. That one was not so easy to remove, being on a curve, and the knife slipped, so she sliced between her finger and thumb. She was wet through in the rain with no coat, but she had to take off her cardigan to wrap it round her cut hand.

In the early days, Jade still used to call round. There were dark roots where before there was honey blonde. Jade always liked to reminisce about the holidays that she and Curtis had taken. Sonya, she had to admit, enjoyed seeing Jade more now than she ever did when she was with Curtis. One night after she had left, Craig said, why is she even bothering coming round here when she is seeing somebody else now?

That's not true, Craig.

Yeah, it is.

But it would be far too soon, Sonya said.

Well, you might think that. Doubt she does.

Jade cancelled coming to the house two weeks in a row. When she eventually did appear, Sonya wasn't wanting to ask.

Sonya, Jade said. No doubt you've heard.

Heard what?

About me.

What about you?

It's nothing serious.

Your life, Sonya said. Up to you.

When Jade left, she told Logan.

He shrugged. Just the way it goes, he said.

She's a skank anyway, said Craig. Curtis could have done way better for himself.

That's enough of that talk, Logan said.

Well, she's a skank. Isn't she, Ma?

It's a relief that there are fewer posters to find these days; it's reassuring going back over roads where she's been before. People defaced them sometimes. They poked out his eyes, or drew glasses on him. She has seen approximations of penises, various shapes and sizes. Curtis wouldn't have been offended by that. She was called into the school once because he had drawn something similar on a textbook. He would probably find it funny.

When a woman in work's son got married, it was all kept very low key. Sonya got asked to the evening do, and she stuck the invitation on the fridge although she'd no intention of going. Just after the funeral they did a fundraiser, a 10k race, and the money went to a mental health charity for young men. Even Sonya ran in the relay, her thighs rubbing together, the tightness in her chest killing her. Next time round though, in a few months, they will be doing it for a premature baby unit.

She has sometimes wondered if she should join Curtis. It has crossed her mind. She went to the doctor's, and he gave her some tablets and suggested a group that met in a school a few miles away. There were a lot of other groups there on the same night. There was line-dancing in the hall, the sound of banjo and pedal steel. She asked a group of women in the hallway what they were there for and it was Spanish conversation. Down the corridor she looked through the square panel of a door. They were in a circle, holding polystyrene cups. There weren't any more seats. She didn't feel like talking anyway, and she didn't feel like listening.

The wooden hoardings around the derelict shop are painted blue. There's a poster for a new club in the town, a list of the DJs and the various nights they are there. There's part of what she thinks is one of Curtis's, but it's already mostly torn off. She is pretty sure that she can see the dark corner of the passport photograph. Hardly worth bothering really but she gets out the water, the scraper and the cloth anyway. Those DJs, that club, Curtis might have enjoyed them. But over there, on the electric box, how could she have missed that one? But it's spanking white. Pristine. Stuck on with new Sellotape. It is not the passport photo. Because it is not a photo of Curtis Rea. It is a photo of Tony McCartan, and he's smiling, leaning against his car in a short-sleeved shirt. Missing since June 17th 2019. The numbers to ring are in dark, bold text beneath.

Sonya is almost indignant. So there's a new guy, another one. Curtis is what, old hat now? The number for the police is different to the one that was on his poster—must be a different area. The electric box is humming and when Sonya looks at Tony McCartan—the edge of his shirt where it touches his arm, the smiling face—the things fall from her hands, the water-bottle and the cloth and the scraper. She sees his mother, getting the posters photocopied, sitting on her son's old bed, folding his old clothes, lying awake in the night. Tony McCartan's mother. The box is vibrating. The air is pounding. Tony McCartan's mother, where is she? Sonya wants to fall into her arms so they can grip each other tight.

Dance Move

A woman Kate knows went to beginners' pole dance. At the end of the six-week course, in addition to a certificate, there was an evening event for family and friends. The studio put a video of it online. Oh no, Kate said. All sorts of people could watch it. Let them, the woman replied, if they've got the inclination. I couldn't care less. Today Kate is watching ballet dancers; the video is titled the top fifteen in the world. A woman on a vast black stage takes demure steps. On to another: a woman in chiffon wisps dances in front of a set with fake stone steps and a fresco. Kate searches for sexual modern ballet to see what comes up. A couple, both in white shirts and black knickers, clinch, disentangle, then clinch again. It's tasteful.

Places in the vicinity offer dance classes, if that's what Clara would like. When Kate phones, they say there are no spots left in beginners' ballet. What about tap? they suggest. No. What about modern dance and hip hop? No, Kate says, more definitely. I'll leave it.

At least Clara's room is now done. Kate assembled the modular bunk and desk herself. She paid double for the decorator to repaper the room on a Saturday morning when everyone else, other than Leon and her, were out. The walls are now a minimal sprig against pale blue. They match the duvet cover. She transferred a couple of her own books to her daughter's shelves, so the bookcase is no longer empty. It's a clean and orderly bedroom for a thirteen-year-old. Alan wondered if she couldn't have consulted Clara on colours or something, let her pick between a couple of wallpaper samples.

When Clara came back that afternoon, Kate said, Look upstairs. Go on, you aren't going to believe it.

Clara went upstairs. And came back down again.

Yeah, you are one hundred per cent right, she said. I don't believe it.

A couple of days later, when Kate went in to pick up the laundry, she saw that, stuck to the wall with a dirty gob of blue-tack, there was a printed image of a man. Smoke billowed from his mouth, his hair was in multi-coloured plaits, and he had rainbow-hued teeth. Among his various facial tattoos was '69' on his forehead, in gothic script. Kate knew this had been run off on her printer because of that big vertical bar of yellow which was always there when the ink was running low. She carefully removed the blue-tack, folded the sheet crisply in two and set it on the desk.

When Clara came into the kitchen to get something to eat, Kate said, Please don't waste those inks.

What do you mean?

Wasting ink. Printing rubbish.

Clara opened the fridge and looked in it.

I think I might phone around, Kate said. For dance classes.

Why not?

Yes. Ballet.

If you fancy it. There's never anything nice to eat in this house.

No. I've been thinking ballet might be good for you to do.

Clara slowly closed the fridge.

Sign yourself up for ballet, she said. I've no interest in doing it. Zero interest in ballet dancing.

And then, within days, another picture of the same person appeared. This time it was a better quality. The man with '69' on his forehead was bare-chested and leaning against a jeep, holding a wad of cash. This time the picture had been stuck on with Sellotape. The cost of that decorator! Kate slid her fingernail, millimetre by millimetre, under the tape. Standing on the threshold, watching her, was Clara.

What are you doing? she asked.

I think you can see what I'm doing.

I printed that in school by the way before the holidays. No need to worry about your inks.

Great the school budget can extend to pupils printing off pictures of undesirables whenever they want.

Kate could see that the bottom right-hand corner was going to rip the wallpaper if she continued to peel.

You finished? Clara asked.

Kate holds Stacey partially to blame. Stacey is always carelessly arranged on a chair or lolling across a worktop. Hi, she says and yawns. What's up? She dumps her bag in their hall, calmly cracks her knuckles at the kitchen table, one, two, three, four, five. And then the other hand. Kate's house, yet Stacey behaves like a queen. That time, Stacey and Clara had gone outside onto the decking. Kate watched what they were up to. Clara shifted a couple of the flower tubs. Hey! Kate was going to say. Leave those where they are! What are you doing? But then Stacey began to move. After a couple of false starts, which resulted in both of the girls bent double laughing, she kicked first one, and then the other leg in the air. Next, she was down on all fours, shaking her behind. And then she lay flat out on the decking, as if she was having sex with it, slapping it on with one hand in encouragement. This was followed by her flicking her legs open, getting on to all fours again, doing the splits in the air and pretending to have sex once more with the decking. That decking had been put down by Kate's dad. That made it worse.

Stacey got up, straightened her sweatshirt and pulled down the cuffs of her tracksuit bottoms, where they had ridden up. She took out her phone and fiddled with it. Kate opened the patio door a little and she heard the music they were moving to, a woman's rhythmic speaking. Now Kate watched as Clara did the same routine. If anything, she was better at it than Stacey, more fluid, more athletic. Then they both did a synchronised version of it. Kate's face was up close to the glass. She must have moved because Stacey looked over and saw her. Stacey smiled and then went to practise one of the transitions from standing to being on the ground. Clara demonstrated to her the way she did it. Then it seemed as though they were watching a video of someone else doing it.

Kate spoke to Alan about it. She said that she had seen some pretty inappropriate behaviour.

Oh, he said. Lucky you.

I'm talking about your daughter. A type of dance.

An inappropriate dance?

Yes, with her friend.

Well, kind of par for the course with that kind of thing. Kids messing. That's why the film's called *Dirty Dancing*.

Dirty Dancing isn't about thirteen-year-olds!

Why were you watching them anyway? The thirteen-year-olds.

Because they moved the plant tubs.

Wee lassie in *Dirty Dancing* was at least seventeen, he said. Seventeen, tops. Called in on my way home with Mark.

How was he?

Good. All good. Same as usual.

He's due a visit from me, she said.

That woman had been unimpressive at pole-dancing when Kate watched the video. Some of the others had managed to get off the ground, but she swung around as if the pole was a lamppost. Even so, there was plenty of applause from friends and family.

The teen mannequin with nylon hair holds a sign saying Back to School although it is still July. She has only one foot and holds a bag with a tennis racquet protruding from it. Kate has insisted they come early. Everything is picked over and dirtied in the town if it's later. The assistant asks them what they want and Kate says that they are in for a new school skirt and a PE kit. The PE kit comes in cellophane bags and the woman says that most people don't bother trying it on. The skirt, however, requires more consideration. She gives Clara two sizes before showing her to the changing room. The liveries of the different schools are there. Kate sees the one where she, Mark and Alan went. That blouse, so stiff, she remembers its collar hard as plastic. Kate goes to the changing room because Clara hasn't appeared yet. She yanks the curtain open.

Do you mind? Clara says.

Hurry up, would you?

She sees Clara is wearing a skirt that fits snugly, showing a slender waist and long, palely muscled legs.

No good, is it? Kate says.

I think it's absolutely fine.

Kate calls over the assistant. Too tight, don't you think? I mean, absolutely.

The assistant is obliged to agree. I suppose if it's bigger she'll be able to grow into it.

Bigger size then, Kate says. Longer and a little looser.

I'll roll it up anyway, Clara says to no one in particular.

Next stop is the shoe shop where Clara says no one goes. Kate lifts a pair from the stand with soles like tractor tread.

No, says Clara.

These will last. Just try them on, Kate says.

When she does, the shoes revel in their ugliness.

Walk over there, Kate says. How do they feel? Do they fit?

Clara doesn't respond.

Kate is aware of a young man working in the shoe shop,

taking furtive glances at Clara as she bends over to tie the laces. Her leggings, when she does that, are no longer opaque. The material, when stretched, shows through its weave the ghost of her pants and where they meet her skin.

We'll take them, Kate says to the assistant.

Are you sure? she asks.

Yeah, I'm sure, she replies.

Kate leaves the new uniform up in Clara's room when they return. Under her arm she also has a cork noticeboard and a hammer. She nails it over the picture of the 69 guy with his cash and his jeep. On the board she pins a piece of paper with all of the days of the week on it. Hardly mind-blowing information, but still. She lifts up the edge of the duvet and looks under the bed. Dirty knickers, their crotches crispy. An empty yoghurt tub next to a book, its pages gluey with it. But nothing else.

It's too late to go to see Mark now. Her brother lives ten miles away. Until recently he lived with a woman called Debbie, but she moved out because they low-level bickered over everything. He says he feels better now she's gone and no, he isn't lonely. His friends, like Alan, have always been good. He's been a best man five, maybe six, times. They always ask him. He went on all of the stag trips. Any of them who were on the holiday that time knew that, on a different night, it could have been them lying immobile, twisted, on the crazy paving beside the swimming pool. They too could have been the one to think, hey lads this will be some laugh, getting from one balcony to the next, you just need to get to the edge, swing with one arm, then catch the other side with your feet, and then—

Those boys, straight from the exam hall, still able to remember their candidate numbers, rangy, awkward with the pretty girls in the hotel disco the night before. Easier just to drink, play-fight each other and jump the balconies. When Kate woke up that morning her mother said there was no one to take her to school because her dad was already at the airport, hoping to get a flight out to Cyprus. Kate would need to get the bus instead.

There followed a few days of people passing in casseroles which lay untouched in the kitchen. Kate helped herself to the packets of sweets kept in the big jar. And then when her mother had to go out to Cyprus too, Kate stayed with the neighbours. She imagined Mark bandaged like a mummy and looking out of the hospital window at a beach. The neighbours put garlic salt over all of their food. Their sheets were never cool. They had fixed cellophane over the windows in one of the rooms so that the sunlight would not fade their settee. It gave everything a gooey yellow light. After four weeks they deemed it safe for Mark to travel and so he was brought home. Home to the hospital, where he would be until after Christmas.

But now Mark works in software design and he can get himself to pretty much any country in the world. He was over six feet by the time he was fourteen, broad too, and impressive. That your brother? they would ask. His legs are folded now and positioned, although that's not always the way. Sometimes he is stretched out on the sofa when she calls round.

Kate's parents live quite close to Mark. They downsized and sold the bungalow. There's some money, her mother said, not a huge amount, but enough to keep you going when we're not here.

Oh please, not the doom and gloom stuff, Kate said.

It's not doom and gloom. It's called reality. And we know you'll always be there for Mark. Isn't that right, Kate?

Well, of course.

It's a consolation to us to know that. That you'll be there for him.

I think that he's doing pretty well, all things considered.

But even so.

I don't know why you would even feel the need to ask me that, she said.

Clara asks if she can go to an under-eighteens dance party being held at the old DIY superstore. It's been transformed into a venue.

No, says Kate.

But you haven't heard anything at all about it.

I don't need to.

But everyone's going.

So what?

It's proper organised. It's not some kind of shady thing.

It'll be full of paedophiles.

Clara goes upstairs and brings down a flyer. You see that? she says. It's under eighteen only. You see that, under eighteen? They don't let paedos in. There will be people at the door to stop the paedos.

Kate looks at excited lettering, the silhouette of a dancer.

Give me that flyer back, Clara said. Let me go and pin it on the board I never asked for.

It's Saturday afternoon and the house is still. Clara is out with friends and earlier Alan left Leon to a kids' party at a soft-play area. Kate watches a romantic film where people, compelled by passion, repeatedly do rash and ridiculous things. Wouldn't have done that, she says to herself. Or that. Or that. And definitely not that. But then, maybe she would have, if she had been in Buenos Aires, where it's set, and had an elaborate confection of a hairdo like the woman in the film and the sound of the tango urged her on. There's a key in the door. She sighs. Alan? she calls. No answer. Alan? There's giggling. She adjusts the sound of the film, but then music comes blaring from the kitchen. Turn that down! she shouts. When there is no change in the volume, she gets up from the sofa and goes in. Did you hear me? she says. Stacey and Clara are sitting on the worktop sucking ice-lollies, inching them in and out of their mouths, between bursts of laughter.

Get down from there, Kate says.

Stacey jumps to the floor. Hi, she says.

Clara gets off the worktop too. We've been in town, she says. Trying on things. Trying them on and then photographing each other in them. Until some woman told us to stop.

Stacey starts laughing. Yeah! Too right she did.

Anyway, says Clara, it's too hot to be in shops on a day like this. We're just going to sit outside for a while.

Kate watches a little more of the film, but she has lost the thread of what is happening. She scrolls through videos of dancing women on her phone. She wonders what the girls are doing in the garden. From the kitchen window she can see them lying on towels that Clara must have taken from the bathroom. They have both pushed the straps of their tops down. Stacey's skirt is in folds around her waist. She moves into the other room where the patio doors are. She sees that they are listening to music, with one headphone each. Clara rolls onto her stomach and says something that makes Stacey laugh. Whatever it is, it makes her pause in conducting the music in the air with her lolly stick.

Kate looks at another fluid spiral of limbs on her phone. And another. Next to the door, Stacey has left her denim jacket. It smells of cleanness. Kate slips her hand into the pocket, where there is only a tissue, folded into four, and a lip balm, an earring in the shape of a daisy. The inside pocket? Only a bus ticket and a sweet wrapper. It's probably too hot for them to do all of their decking booty-shaking today. That place that did the course in pole dancing, sure, some were alright after six weeks, but they weren't wonderful. But there's no doubt that, setting aside the sleazy aspect, it requires tremendous upper body strength. She is sure that these others, in that respect, are highly impressive. Here's a woman in fake moonlight almost climbing the air. She watches another video and another.

When the doorbell rings, it's Leon, pink and sweaty from the party. Kate waves and says 'thanks' to a parent who drives off without seeing her. Leon runs out into the back garden with a shout, and the two girls get up to start chasing him. Stacey grabs the hose and Clara turns on the tap. They run after Leon who doesn't move very fast because it would seem he wants to be soaked. Then Stacey lifts him up onto her back and scoots around the garden as Clara whoops and chases with the hose.

Kate opens the door.

Stop that, she says. Stop that, you're wasting water. And you're making a mess.

Clara stands still. How can a hose make a mess? she asks.

It just does.

So why have a hose?

Because if you use a hose appropriately, that's alright, but what you're doing is making a mess.

Stacey turns off the tap so that the water coming out of the hose diminishes to a trickle. But then there are a final couple of belated spurts. Both of the girls laugh.

That looks kinda… wrong! Clara says.

Yeah, that looks kinda wrong, parrots Leon.

Right that's it, inside please, Leon, Kate says. Inside, now. Girls, would you make sure that you leave that hose exactly as you found it?

Sure, says Stacey. Sorry.

Okay, let's return the hose to its appropriate position, says Clara.

When she goes to visit Mark, Kate always brings Leon. He loves the apartment and its gadgets. Why can't we have? he begins, before a glance from Kate silences him. Mark's bed has a control that allows it to rise up and down, almost fold itself in half. As soon as they arrive, Leon asks Mark if he can have a go on it.

Mark, as usual, says, Go ahead.

You want me to make us a coffee? Kate asks, also as usual.

Nope, just give me a couple of minutes here.

And then she will go into the kitchen to carry the cups through to the living room.

So how's things? he asks.

Fine. Endless round of birthday parties for your man. She nods in the direction of the bedroom. Never done buying presents. My go to is a Nerf gun. Don't know if that's meant to be appropriate these days. Buying kids guns.

Don't know. What else should you buy?

A book or something.

Don't think they'd thank you for that. The kids.

A book about how to explore the flora and fauna in your back garden.

Stick with the Nerf gun, Kate.

So yeah, plenty going on with Leon, Kate says. And I think Clara is going to start ballet soon. But I still need to get it sorted out.

Okay, he says. You know who I'm seeing next week? You know who's going to be over? Glenn. Glenn Evans. Seeing his folks.

She knew Glenn Evans and his parents. Their two families had ended up spending a lot of time together after the accident. They even went on holiday together, although that word was a misnomer. Sleeping on a bunk bed in a spartan room in a godforsaken part of the country and doing archery and canoeing in the rain: there were other terms for that. Their parents met through the organisation that supported the families. There was also Anita, a pretty girl with red hair who had suffered a spinal stroke that left her paralysed.

Glenn was injured when a scrum collapsed during a school rugby match. He was a year younger than Mark. The Evanses hadn't had to move house like Kate's family, whose tall and skinny terrace was no good. In the old house the putty around the windows was old and cracked. The glass, when it was windy, felt like it would blow in. The house always felt slightly dangerous, precarious. The new bungalow was warm, quiet, double-glazed. There was a built-in wardrobe in her room where all of her stuff was hidden.

So yeah, Mark says. Will be good to see him, see what he's up to these days.

Mrs Evans said all the time, but he's our only child, he's all we have. She was angry: with schools, with sports programmes, with balls, with grass. It hadn't been Glenn's fault in the way that with Mark, even though it was bad luck, it really was, the drunk and reckless boy. Mrs Evans sometimes sat with her mum. They nursed coffees, the radio quiet in the background, as they talked about hospitals and rehabilitation and the research that there was in the States. They had their favourite doctors. They bitched about Anita's parents who they thought weren't proactive enough in her rehabilitation. Kate knew how she had to behave. When anyone asked about Mark, she said, brightly, he's doing fine. In school they had a fundraiser and she had to get her photo taken with the giant cheque. It was embarrassing. She heard Mark cry in the night sometimes, which made her cry too, but she said nothing.

She never asked anyone to come to the house because she didn't want them staring at him, or the paraphernalia that was in place for him. So no one invited her in return. But anyway, there was an air of tragedy about her which spoiled the vibe. People didn't want to do stupid, goofy things around someone who knew how wrong those could go. She heard the stories on Monday morning of the things they all did. They went to an industrial estate where there was an old and derelict cigarette factory. It was massive, cavernous, and loads of kids from other schools went too. The police never hassled anyone for drinking; they never came anywhere near it. Her family went to bed early, every night of the week. Mark had his physio first thing in the morning.

For sure, Kate said. Where is it he lives now? Glasgow?

Just outside. Yeah.

Will be nice.

Still a big rugby fan.

Oh, is he?

Not so long after Mark had the accident, Kate's mum stopped using make-up. An ascetic, scrubbed face was more appropriate to the situation. All frivolous stuff, eye-palettes with their nightclub shades, dozens of lipsticks, were reclaimed by Kate. Her fourteen-year-old peach cheeks needed no foundation, but she put it on, and did her lips like a fifties pin-up. Her mum ditched clothing too. Kate got some patent high heels and a jumper dress that hung off her shoulder. She twirled in front of the mirror, tried out a range of expressions.

She imagined Brendan there, sitting on her bed. Brendan had been an instructor on one of those holidays: canoeing, archery, swimming. The younger guys, doing work experience for university, took their orders from him. He had a slow, unconcerned amble.

One afternoon, she hadn't gone canoeing. She'd said she had a headache and it was half true. It was that close, heavy weather, but she was fed up with sitting in water. She watched them from the lounge area with its rack of magazines and big yellow sofas. Brendan came over and looked out of the window too. You didn't want to join them? he asked. She shook her head, embarrassed, not knowing what to say. He took her hair and twisted it round his hand. It felt adult. You're really pretty, he said. He tilted her face so she was looking up at him. Thanks very much, she said, not knowing what else would suit in the circumstances. His other hand moved towards her face and he touched her mouth with his thumb.

Yeah, you are, he said.

Thanks very much, she said again.

When he let his hand drop, it brushed her chest. She wondered if he had done it by accident. Then one of the other instructors came in, and her hair fell again to her shoulders. That night with Anita's younger sister in the bunk below her, reading aloud from a picture book, Kate thought again about the details, as she twisted her own hair, letting her hand drop too. She was frightened to see him the next day, their final one. Men weren't meant to do things like that. But she was looking forward to it too, and so was disappointed, a little, when she only caught sight of him in the distance, working on a trailer.

But still, it was to him that she talked in that bedroom when everyone else was asleep and she was there, in the make-up and the jumper. She put on headphones and danced in front of the mirror.

You're very pretty, he said.

Yes, I suppose I am, aren't I?

You're very pretty.

Yes, I am, and what you gonna do about it?

You're very pretty.

Leon comes in from the bedroom. Can we go out the back, Uncle Mark? he asks.

Sure, he says, I am gonna whip your ass this time, let me tell you that.

Kate looks out the window as they throw the ball to each other, Mark throwing it so that Leon has to dive to catch it, but Leon always making sure that it comes within Mark's reach.

She imagined him in her bedroom for many years of her teens. It was strange to see him one day in town, coming out of a shop with an old woman with a walking frame who Kate took to be his mother. He was balding. Kate held the door open to let them past. He nodded and murmured thanks. He didn't recognise her. It was just before she got married. She remembered that the first time Alan touched her, Alan, who had elided from Mark's friend, to his visitor, to her boyfriend, to her husband almost imperceptibly, she thought of Brendan that day, looking out at the canoes.

Eventually Kate shouts to Leon to come in. They need to go. He runs to the cupboard where Mark has always got a chocolate bar for him to take home.

*

You've just missed them, Alan says, when they return. The girls. They're away on out.

Away on out where?

Clara and Stacey. They're away to the rave.

But I told her that she couldn't go! You knew that! We'd agreed.

Had we? Can't say I remember that, baby.

Alan is trying to get the lawnmower to work. He pulls the cord but nothing happens.

This thing, he says. It's useless.

What was she dressed like?

Haven't a clue, Kate.

We said that it wasn't appropriate for her. And that she shouldn't go.

Well, I can't remember what we said, but fact is, she's there now. So, you know, end of story. He pulls the lawnmower cord again but there's silence.

That's just terrific, Kate says.

She's there now and I'll pick them up at eleven when it finishes. We actually might need to buy a new one of these.

No, says Kate.

Okay, Kate, if you think you're a bit of a pro when it comes to lawnmowers. If you think you're going to be able to sort this out. Be my guest.

No, I'll pick them up. I'll do it.

He pulls the cord again.

Sure, he says. Whatever suits, but you know, I actually think this thing has had its day. I think we are looking at a new lawnmower.

*

When she leaves the house that night, the heat has given way to a cool calm. Kate pulls a light jumper over her T-shirt, and slopes out to the car in baggy jogging bottoms and the old slippers that are almost outdoor wear. As she gets into the car, she sees Leon's big wall light giving the room a green glow. He'll have been asleep for hours, lying with the duvet half off him. In the town at the crossing, she has to wait because it takes three women so long to totter across in their heels. They mouth an apology to her and she silently says, it's okay. Because it is okay. She isn't going to give Clara a hard time. She will without complaint give Stacey a lift home to wherever that might be. And, when she comes back home, she will sit with Alan and have a glass of wine, with the patio doors open, looking out onto a half-cut back garden in the dark.

Alan said that the arrangement was that they should meet him in the car park of the place, the old DIY superstore, just after eleven. Kate has already sent Clara a text to let her know she is on her way. When she turns into the entrance, she remembers that they bought a table and chairs here once. She recalls the difficulty of getting the flat-packs into the boot, the trial and error of different configurations. There's a ghost space where the big orange initials of the shop used to be, and over near the hedge where she parks, there's a pole, its top lopped off, the sign gone. She messages Clara again, this time more snippily. I am here, she says. Where are you? Kate turns round when a group of teenagers walk by, but they are there and then gone. They have disappeared into the night. No reply to the message. She puts down the window and hears the noise coming from the old superstore, insistent and faster than a heartbeat. Kate drums her fingers on the steering wheel. How long is she expected to wait? She looks at the guts of an old sofa that someone has dumped beside the old, smashed shelter for the trolleys. And then, unceremoniously, the lights in the carpark go out. Well that's it. She gets out of the car and walks over to the entrance. Another mother is waiting and they exchange sympathetic smiles. The things we do for our kids, right? Then three boys appear for her, skinny, in T-shirts. They too go into the darkness. Kate tries to ring Clara but there is no answer.

She goes to where they used to sell flowers and grow bags. How much longer is this due to go on? she asks one of the men in black bomber jackets.

Another half hour max, he says.

Kate isn't waiting another half hour max.

Okay, she says. Thanks very much.

She waits until one of the men is on his phone, and the other is talking to some kids who have lost a bag. A couple of young women are at the entrance too, both with ear pieces, but they don't notice her. It's the end of the night and they look bored. They do not see Kate slip by. A young guy does and he shouts at her, Hey this is under eighteens, love. Oi, love! But she doesn't turn to look at him because she is entering the hall where blades of light illuminate on off, on off, a sea of heads bobbing up and down.

She is taken aback by it, the loudness of the music which she can feel in the pit of her stomach, but also the movement of what is in front of her, this thing, like one organism, that she stares at. All the hands are in the air and the place is bathed, suddenly, in yellow and pink. She looks down at her jogging bottoms and slippers. They're here, somewhere, the girls, and she wants to go home. A teenage girl in shorts has her eyes closed, the music weaving through her. Kate feels her legs heavy as she tries to move past people to get to the perimeter, to put her back against the cool wall. Nowhere is there Clara's face. All these limbs, everywhere, liquid, and loose. Even the plaster behind her seems to be pounding. Through the people she sees someone laughing and pointing and it is Stacey. There's Clara beside her and Stacey is getting her to look over. It's your mum! she mouths. She beckons Kate to join them. Come on! Come over! The little group has made a space. The blades of light are changing colour and the air is throbbing. And Kate, she waves back, but she cannot move.

Gloria and Max

Max Haynes had been in Northern Ireland for just under two months: long enough to know its limitations. Those presented themselves within two days, such as the cultural quarter of Belfast that consisted of a single street. He was there as visiting professor of film. And now he was in his car, driving to a place in the middle of nowhere.

There was to be a film festival in some godforsaken spot and he had been roped in to attending a planning meeting. Yeah, for sure, he could appreciate the importance of an outreach dimension to the work of the faculty. He had in fact already programmed a short Unknown Pleasures series for the university cinema based on Slavic mythology. And as far as he was concerned, it had been quite a success. Yet the prospect of this small local festival filled him with little enthusiasm. Indeed, it presented significant ideological and aesthetic issues because—as a festival of so-called Christian cinema—it was mono-cultural and reductive. But nonetheless Max had agreed to go. And he had also said that he would give a lift to another attendee, a woman called Gloria, who would be waiting outside the Spar in one of the unfortunate little places he had to pass through.

It was, however, very pleasant going along in the car, through red and yellow trees. In London or the other cities where he'd lived, Max had rarely driven at all. But on arrival for the new, temporary job, they'd offered car leasing. He'd laughed at first and gone to the showroom reluctantly, but when he went for the test-drive in the sleek and stately machine, that was it. He joked about it to Janika when he sent her a photo of it. So not me! he said. But, still, he had gone for the impressive car.

Max arrived at the designated place at the agreed time. It was not a particularly attractive spot. Although it felt rural, the huge chimney of a nearby power station loomed through the trees. In this main street he wondered if people were waiting for some kind of drugs drop, such were the numbers loitering. Three teenage guys were taking turns to jump on the silver inflatable from the inside of a wine box. Behind them was a sign advertising hot food. A burrito wore a sombrero and had a moustache. That was fairly typical of the place. He would hesitate to brand everyone in the country rednecks because many weren't. Max had met several people at the university that he would certainly keep in touch with after he left at the end of the year. And there was the guy and his partner who did film scores. But undoubtedly there were also a lot of rednecks.

At the bus stop in front of the shop a crowd of girls waited. Two women stood talking together as a dog on a lead gyred round. One of the boys kicked the burrito sign. On the other side of the street there was a funeral director's with an outsize drum clock above the window, its slow hand performing its sweep. Max cringed at its clumsiness.

And then, turning back, he saw a heavy-set, middle-aged woman in jeans, white trainers and a pale pink anorak. She had patchy short blonde hair and looked entirely unperturbed as she stood against the front of the shop.

Max wondered how this woman might feel about being in a car, an enclosed space, with a man she didn't know. It might make her feel less uneasy if he banged on a bit about Janika. That would establish that he wasn't a threat, and that Janika was a person who, if not there in physical manifestation, was constantly there in thought.

Max rolled down the window.

Gloria! he said, not loud enough. Gloria! he shouted. It sounded ridiculous, like some kind of dreadful Van Morrison tribute act. Gloria!

The woman looked over, unconcerned, and then walked towards the car.

Hi, he said, once she had got in beside him, I'm Max, and even though I have no idea how to get to this place I've got the satnav to help us.

It's a straight road, Gloria said. To get there.

That's good to know, Max said. But he kept the satnav on.

So, Max said, here we are on our way to this planning meeting. You're very interested in film?

Gloria considered this, and then said, Well, I watch a few things on the telly. Now and again.

Well, film's actually what I'm involved in, Max said.

You make films? Gloria asked.

No, I teach film at the university.

Oh, she said.

I'm a film academic.

Oh. Film academic. Teaching the people about films.

Yes.

How to make films?

No. How to watch them.

Lesson one. How to turn on the TV, she said, looking out the window of the car.

I've just moved to Belfast, Max began. But actually, my partner is still in London. Well, she's from Finland, originally, but she's in London.

Okay, Gloria said.

Yeah, said Max. She's called Janika. The distance makes no difference really. Not that we're really so very far away from each other, not really. Belfast and London. We're, you know, very in love.

Gloria rearranged the hood of her anorak where it had got caught in the seat-belt.

Yeah, said Max.

Okay, said Gloria.

So what's your involvement then with this festival? Max asked.

Mr Anderson said for me to go, she replied. Mr Anderson's the boss of my place. He's the boss of all the homes. They're going to be bringing all the old people from the homes to see the films.

That's gonna be some job, she added.

And what type of films do you expect that the old people will like?

Old ones? Gloria said. She looked round the car. You picking anyone else up?

No, just you, Gloria.

The cars flashed by in the other lane. There was a buzz in the car from a fly. It crawled along the dashboard and then flew off to land again on the dashboard.

Where is the home where you work then? Max asked.

On the way out of Carrick, she said.

Max smiled. Well that's dependent really on which way you came into Carrick, isn't it?

Gloria paused. If you don't know whether you're coming in or out of Carrick, there's not a lot of hope for you, she said.

The smell of her was in the car, despite its newness and the air-conditioning. He couldn't place it. An astringent lemon, like a shower gel, but also something else, like dogs. He could imagine her walking a couple of muscled terriers early in the morning. He looked across and saw the nails cut short, the weathered hands.

And do you not drive, Gloria? he asked.

I do, she said. But Billy takes the car.

That's your partner?

Husband. Billy takes the car.

Billy has the prerogative to take the car?

He needs it to get to work, she said.

And when do you go out in the car?

When he doesn't need to get to work.

When Max had been young they had a woman who came to tidy up, not a cleaner. There was a certain insouciance to tidying up; it suggested sorting books into piles, folding some newspapers, and she did that too, but it probably didn't give a sense of mopping dirt, which was what she also did. One week she didn't arrive and then the next, when she did, she was apologetic, the side of her face pale yellow and green. His mother had given her an address and a purse full of money. But the woman left the purse on the little table beside the door. Two weeks later she didn't turn up again and they had had to let her go because they needed someone reliable. Max thought he wouldn't enquire any further about Gloria's husband Billy.

A lorry overtook them, sending pieces of stone up to hit the windscreen. Max turned on the radio. Two men were talking about emerging financial markets in the Far East.

How do you feel, Max said, batting at the fly, about this being a specifically Christian film festival?

Gloria shrugged. Old people wouldn't want smut, she said.

It's either smut or Christian, do you think? Max asked.

There was talk of them showing the film about the runners, Gloria said. *Chariots of Fire*. The fella doesn't want to run on a Sunday. And so he doesn't.

Most places are open now on a Sunday, she went on. Wonder what he'd think of that. Not much.

Max wondered if someone else would be able to give Gloria a lift home.

Me and my friend, she said. My friend worked in a video shop on the Shore Road and I would keep her company. Derelict now, but it's one of the fake shops, got the hoardings up to take the bad look off it. They've made it look like it's a shoe shop.

Haven't noticed any places like that.

There was the throb of a motorbike as it sped past them.

They're everywhere, well.

The satnav was showing that Max needed to make a left turn. He slowed down in anticipation, put on the indicator.

No, said Gloria. That's not the way.

That's where I'm being told to go.

Not the way. But, she said, it's up to you.

They turned up a narrower road in between high hedges. There was a gradient before it plateaued out.

It was only small, Gloria said, but a lot of people came into that video shop. A lot of men. Have you anything else out the back? some of them would ask. I'm sure you know what I mean. But we were only teenagers. We didn't want to go looking around out the back for dirt. Not for those men anyway. The place we're heading to, it used to be somewhere you could get ice-creams. And then before that it was a dancehall.

Max didn't reply.

We might be late, you know, going this way, Gloria said.

Is that what you always wanted to do, Gloria—work in an old people's home?

Gloria gave a slow sigh. Then she turned to look out of the window, as she wound the drawstring of her hood around her finger.

It's just a job, she eventually said, as she slipped out her finger and let the string unspool. Just a job, like you watching the films at the university.

Well, said Max, what I would say is that—

And then, up in front, in the middle of the road, was something shiny and twisted. Max pulled on the brakes. It was the motorbike, mangled, the wheel buckled. There was a stink of petrol and burnt rubber. It had hit a tree, and the wood exposed by the impact was naked white. Gloria and Max were out of the car. Gloria pointed further down the road to a crumple on the grass verge. And then they were there looking down at a young man. The helmet was cracked open. His legs were in black jeans and he wore trainers. Gloria knelt down beside him.

Still alive, she said to Max.

To the young man she said, I've got you. She had taken off his black glove and was holding his hand.

Phone 999, she told Max.

He went to go back to the car to get his phone. No—use mine, Gloria said.

I've got you, Gloria said to the boy.

Emergency services asked Max the name of the road but he didn't know and had to ask Gloria. She took the phone from him.

On the front of Gloria's pink anorak, there was a streak of blood. Max felt vomit rise in his throat. This was a bizarre place, with its hawthorn trees and the broken body of the young man on the ground, his own car grotesque and sinister in the late winter sunlight. And then Gloria let go of the hand so that it sat pale on the edge of the leather jacket. She wiped the back of her hand across her face and looked down at her knees. The police and ambulance came within ten minutes, which to Max had seemed vast, an eternity. Gloria gave a short statement to a policewoman.

When they got into the car they didn't speak.

Finally, Gloria spoke. Might as well give that Christian cinema a miss then, she said.

Max put the key in the ignition and the engine turned over, but the car didn't move. He switched it off again.

I'm sorry, he said. Sorry.

Gloria reached across and put her hand on his arm. She let it rest there until he put the car into gear. They didn't utter a single word on the journey back to the shop with the Mexican sign outside.

Thanks for the lift, Gloria said as she got out, the blood on the pink anorak now rust.

A year later Max was living back in London, his visiting professorship over. Janika's parents had lent them the money for a deposit on a small but sleek house. They would sometimes reminisce about the relative trials of their 'long-distance' relationship, and occasionally, when they had friends round, Janika might say, tell them about that festival thing. And he would be articulate about the absurdity of the Christian film festival, and why the journey was aborted, without really mentioning Gloria at all. He didn't say that, at least a couple of nights a week, as he lay in the room beside Janika, the bed warm with the scent of her perfume, he thought of the roll of an engine, a stained pink anorak, her hand on his arm.

Bildungsroman

Even on the morning of his wedding Lee texted her, because it was the allotted day. Under the dome of the atrium, a marble pillar concealed him as he tapped out the usual message. Still there? The reply came almost immediately. Still there. An agitated bridesmaid rustled by. Why wasn't he over where he needed to be, for the photographer?

When they posted the list, Lee was the only one further afield. Why him, for fuck's sake? He went straight to McCallum's room and burst in, no knock. Can I help you? McCallum said. Can't make it. I'm telling you now, it's too far away, Lee said. Less than twenty miles, McCallum replied. You're seventeen. What you frightened of? Young boy all alone in the big city? You're being asked to go down a motorway to do a short work placement. And no, I cannot get you somewhere else. Difficult enough finding you boys anywhere without chopping and changing. Bus there and back, job done. But know what, if you think you can sort yourself out with another placement somewhere, then feel free to use my phone, son. He leaned back in his chair. Feel free to use my phone.

The guy says you have to stay in a hotel? his mother said. Really? Is he kidding?

Lee had taken some time to assess the situation. The buses didn't go early or late enough and they had told them to expect irregular shifts. If he had to go, it made a lot of sense to stay in a hotel, a place with a balcony where he could look out over the city, having a smoke, columns of light from the sky scrapers. A TV would emerge from the bottom of the bed at the press of a button. Knock on the door. See who it is. Girl spilling out of a bikini. Come on in. I got Cristal. I got, well, other expensive drinks too. Not sure of the names of them. A hotel? his mother said. You sure he didn't mean a hostel? Well he was not staying with a bunch of homeless guys, no fucking way. But she said she meant a youth hostel, for people globetrotting. No, the guy said absolutely nothing about people globetrotting.

Yeah, Lee said to the boys. Could say I lucked out big time. Hot older woman. You know what they are like. Gagging for it. They asked if he had any pics and he said, not yet. But give him time. His mother gave instructions: no smoking, always say please and thank you. Anything needing done, do it with good grace. She had been talking about his work placement with their neighbour and he had said that his sister lived in Belfast. There would be no problem for Lee to stay with Eileen. Please, thank you, Your Grace. Is this some kind of upper-class person? he asked.

In fact, no problem if Eileen was upper class. In the college there was a poster of a beautiful older woman holding a laptop and two books. It said underneath, with a big curvy question mark, *Returning To Education?* She looked slick and wealthy and none too interested in Food Preparation Level 2 or Level 3 Carpentry. He knew he was definitely not the only person who had tossed off thinking about her in the ground floor toilets, even though there were no locks on the doors. Get that sorted, you guys! She put down the laptop and two books before taking her kit off and he handed them back to her afterwards.

As his bus approached Belfast on the Sunday night, however, the prospect of Eileen became somewhat terrifying. But not entirely so: he had looked up what mature women liked and according to the website there were three main things. Number one: good communication. They had done units on that in school. You start with a topic sentence, something like that. Use adjectives and all that shit. If you're talking, don't mumble. Number two was, he couldn't remember. But three was they liked to take it slow. Well, that was fine. He could manage that.

The address was written on a piece of lined paper, and as the taxi headed to it, they passed houses with grand gardens, some even striped two shades like a football pitch. But things began to shrink, the cars and the homes, until they stopped at a small semi at the end of a cul de sac. There was a hanging basket outside with nothing in it, and when he rang the bell, no one answered. He checked the paper. Yeah, right number. He rang the bell again. This time, through the pebbled glass, a beige shape appeared and disappeared. Oh my god, surely she wasn't naked already? No way. He took a step back from the doorstep, unsure of what to do. Then the fragmented beige appeared again. Getting closer. Getting closer so that it filled up most of the glass. The door opened and there was a scrawny individual in a washed-out tracksuit. She looked out onto the street, as if expecting someone else to be there, before closing the door.

Everything was grey and white in the living room, apart from a massive leather chair the colour of a strawberry ice cream. Chilly old place. On the mantelpiece there was a vase of stalks. He wondered if she was religious. But then she asked him if he wanted a beer. She wasn't sure, she said, if young people drank beers these days. He had fairly swiftly decided that no, he couldn't fancy her at all. He looked all over her for a curve and couldn't find one. Her mouth was frayed at the ends, the skin cracked. At home he stared at smiling versions of himself, one from every year. His mother always bought the school photos in their brown paper frames. Here just the walls looked back. He said that he didn't want a beer, so she took him upstairs to the box room where he would sleep, the rolled up sleeping bag sitting on a sponge chair that folded out to be a bed. She closed the door behind her. He took his suit out of the bag, like his mother had said. Then he opened the window, sat up on the sill and smoked some of the little bit he had brought with him. In the back garden there was the skeleton of an old rotary washing line. He looked at his phone: just one of the boys asking about how hot this older woman actually was. He found a picture of a topless woman who looked over thirty. So fucked already dunno if I am even gonna make it to da work! Fuck dat anyway life is for da livin!

In his bag there was a box of chocolates and a little

card for Eileen from his mother. He should give them to her. When he handed them over, he asked if there was anything that she wanted him to do. Good grace and all of that fucking shit. She asked if he would like a chocolate. The corner of the box was dented from where it had hit the bus window when he swung his bag. He watched her while she tried to pull open the cellophane. Maybe try one of the corners, he said. She said she would get a knife from the kitchen, and she did, a big serrated bread knife which sliced through cellophane and cardboard. There, she said, at long last, and he took the one with the nut.

The next morning, he left the house early to get the two buses to the industrial estate. He hadn't wanted to talk to Eileen, who would have been getting ready to go to her job in the garage. He was tired, that bed was uncomfortable, and it had sounded like old Eileen was up half the night, banging about, lights on, lights off, and even the ceiling seemed to creak. Guys in jail in the old films, they scored off the days of their sentence on the wall. Put a line through Sunday in a big fat squidgy marker. Only another four nights to go.

He arrived in his suit at the reception office that had, behind the desk, the name of the company in slanted aluminium letters. When the woman inquired who he was there to see, he said, uh, the boss? On determining that he was one of the work experience youngsters, she sent him to Warehouse 3 where he was to ask for Gerry. Warehouse 3 was cavernous; birds even twittered in the highest reaches. He had known which one it was by the huge white 3 that seemed to float on the metal siding. The men sitting on palettes turned to look at him. Sharp dressed man, one said. You still got the price on that suit? Lee said he was there to speak to Gerry but they said there was no one there called that. Maybe he meant Terry. Terry was over there, in a windowed-off part of the warehouse. As he walked over to Terry, one of the guys made a noise like a chicken. When the man came out and said, you're the young fella, have you got your paperwork? Lee said, I do indeed, Terry. Gerry, the man said. He gave him a piece of paper with the hours he was to work written on it. You'll be doing nothing heavy, he said, because they didn't want to have to take him to casualty. He gave him a laminated set of instructions and said when he had studied them he should go back to where he had come from to speak to Hendo. So that's Hendo and not Bendo? Lee said. The man looked at him. I want you to read those instructions, he said. This was a twenty-four-hour operation, shifting objects all over the world. It was precision. But as he walked over to the men on the palettes, Lee looked at his hours. There were no late nights apart from Wednesday. And he could make it in the mornings if he got the earliest bus. That didn't seem a bad prospect, getting up early, not after a night with Eileen.

The man who had said about the suit was Hendo. He told Lee that there was a glitch in the computer inventory and that his job was to count the packs of small components in the D area. He gave him the printout of a spreadsheet. Lee remembered that the assignment he was meant to do was on the brand identity of the company. It was boring to count and the numbers were the same most of the time as on the sheet. These pieces of metal, wrapped in plastic, they would taste like blood. A man once ate a bike. He was from France. Monsieur something or other. He ate other shit too. He could probably eat all of these components. An all-you-can-eat metal buffet, this place would be to him.

Hendo gave him a shout when it was lunchtime. They went to a portacabin that had a table and a kettle and an old TV. They ate out of lunchboxes. He hadn't thought to bring anything because he assumed there would be a café or restaurant for the workers. Even at the college there was a snack bar! One of the others, when he saw that Lee had nothing, offered him half a sandwich, said, you want that? The big guy with the accent was eating boiled eggs and a sliced chicken breast. Can't be right, Hendo said. Eating something at two stages of its life. It's like fucking a mother and daughter at the same time, one of the other men observed. The others laughed, so Lee did too. Just maxing my protein, the big guy said good-naturedly. That's all. In the afternoon, Lee stacked boxes that had arrived on a lorry. He wouldn't ever do work like this anyway. Fair enough, putting stuff on the shelves if you are a sixteen-year-old in a part-time job, that's how it works, but anybody doing that kind of thing when they were older was an A-grade loser, and no doubt about it. He'd have a Porsche Carrera at some point, no a Lotus Elise, no a Maserati, no a Lamborghini. Fuck da shelves!

Later it took Eileen a long time to come to the door again. He had turned to go, thinking she was out, before he saw the movement through the glass. When she made the tea that evening, she stood by the cooker to eat hers, rather than sit at the table with him. He wondered if she was one of those women who had been beaten up by guys, assaulted by them, and was frightened now of even a teenager like him. In fact, maybe having him to stay in her house was Eileen's worst nightmare. It was the phone call from hell, the one saying that he was going to come to stay. There was a woman singing on the radio, a romantic song. That's kind of a good tune, isn't it? he said. He wanted to appear unthreatening, a fella who listened to women singing. She has a good voice, he added. Eileen said that she thought it was a hit a while ago. But she didn't move any closer. That evening he watched videos on his phone while she sat downstairs. Later, there was more banging and scuttling. Maybe mice were in the roof space, or rats.

The next day he didn't wear a suit and he bought a sandwich at a garage. Also, he had to work with a guy called Tommy. Tommy said that he wasn't going to get home until late. He had to go to the city centre. To see a solicitor. He had crashed into someone, but he had no insurance and he wasn't taxed. He thought sometimes about moving to Scotland. His brother was there and he had his own business, sanding and staining, in Paisley. He was doing really well. He could work for him. Change of scene. What's sanding and staining? Lee asked. Floors, Tommy said. Well, why don't you then? Lee asked, although to him floors didn't sound like escape to paradise. Tommy said it was because he had a two-year-old son in Belfast. That meant he couldn't leave. Wasn't with the mother any more, that's how it went, but he didn't want to leave. Tommy taped closed another cardboard box. Sometimes you just got to put up with things. Best you can do. You have no choice. Lee said nothing about the man and his son. Another day gone and he had done nothing yet on brand identity. Nobody seemed to care too much about brand identity.

Eileen had, on this evening, quartered some tomatoes to put next to the meal she had bought. She sat at the table this time and asked him how the work was going. He said that it was fine but that tonight would be his last night with her because they didn't need him to work late any days. He could go home. She nodded and didn't seem displeased. They ended up sitting in the living room. He watched a film about gangsters in Chicago on his phone, with the sound turned down low. It was historical. She read a magazine about celebrities. He saw her looking over at him every so often but he concentrated on the film, even though it wasn't that interesting. He'd seen it before. When she finished the magazine, she went back to the front cover and read it again.

That night was hot and the bed like a coffin. They were walking about, up above him, the people at his funeral, and he wondered how he would die, an ancient happy man who maybe knew karate or other martial arts and who was chilled to fuck after living a long life. Or maybe, killed in a car crash next year, a sudden twist of metal. A beam of light showed under the door, a skinny light sabre. Right that was it. Lee was getting up. When he opened the door, he saw on the landing a silver ladder leading to a black square hole in the ceiling. The metal, as he ascended, was cold on his bare feet. A single bare bulb clipped to a beam lit the place. There was Eileen on her knees in front of a black bin bag. A couple of steps and he was standing behind her. She was looking at something that was in an old shoebox. It was a handgun.

He gave a fake cough, and Eileen turned round, a panicked grim reaper in a black fleece dressing gown. She let out a frightened shape of a sound. Please don't tell, she said. Please don't tell anyone. Please don't. You mustn't say. And she put the lid on the box and pushed it under the bin bag. He asked if it was a replica and she said yes. Is the… replica loaded? he asked and she said that she didn't know. Don't touch it, don't touch it! but he had already taken the box from under the plastic and, using the arm of a silky yellow blouse that was in the bin-bag, he lifted the gun carefully. He knew that was what you did. He'd seen it so many times on the TV. He took aim at the small square of light where he had come from, the other arm of the blouse dangling.

Eileen, is this yours? he asked. Tons of people had real guns in their houses, legally held shotguns and whatnot. Because anybody who had ever been in the police, even for a couple of months, they were allowed to hold on to the gun as a kind of free gift. That was fact. She said for him to put it back and she pointed at the rafters as if they could hear, and so he said, alright don't worry. Back it went in the shoe box, and the blouse was returned to the bin bag.

When they both had gone down the ladder, Eileen folded it and took it to her bedroom, before saying goodnight to him. Lee lay back again on the bed. One of his boys had messaged him with a video of a man getting chased by a bull. He clicked on an advert for a pizza with a new type of base, then went back again to watching the guy running across the field. The light was still there, seeping under the door. Then a knock came. He ignored it and closed his eyes. I don't want to disturb you, Eileen said, but are you awake? He rolled over to face the wall. Lee, you won't say to anyone? Lee? Eileen, you can chill, he said. I'm not a tout. The door opened and he felt her weight on the sponge bed.

She'd never been in trouble with the police in her life, she said, and it was very important he didn't mention anything to anyone because she would get locked up for it. Alright, he said, that's no bother, like I said. He looked at his phone to see what the time was, but managed to hit play on the advert for the pizza. A man was talking about the crust. Nu Yo-ik style! he declared. Sorry, Lee said. But still she sat there. Hard to know where to start, she began. Well no need to start at all, he offered, hoping that she wouldn't but knowing, from the way the silence was pressing in on him, that she would. She said that Ivan left, and maybe that was where it began. He met a woman with red hair and I said stay, you could even see her if you want to, but please, just stay. He said no, that wouldn't be fair on anyone. But I wasn't asking for fair. She said that what came when Ivan left was a darkness even on the brightest afternoon of the week. I felt it here, and he supposed she was pointing to some part of herself, her heart or maybe her head. Did you ever think, Lee began, about just having a drink? I don't mean going overboard. One or two. Might not be your thing but you possibly could've got a bit of a chill just smoking some, you know, cannabis.

He remembered that boy, Benjy Hughes, a kind of semi-friend, with the scab on the inside of his arm, how he had rubbed it with a coin. It was nearly like jelly one day and he asked him, the guy who was actually a really good centre-mid, why the fuck are you doing that? And Benjy Hughes said, with a shrug, I just do. He didn't really understand what anyone else was doing. He hardly knew what he was doing himself.

But then, Eileen said she got a calm. Got a calm. And it came through something so simple. She started buying, and she started buying all kinds of stuff. Things that could be put in a bag or lifted out of a box, delivered, that made the place nice, that said you are something. The looking for the things, the searching for them, touching them, it took up her time. Some stuff she bought was beautiful and some a waste of money, but it didn't matter. Lee wondered where the beautiful stuff had gone because this place with its stalks in vases was not by any means a palace. The gun but, Lee said. Did he leave it behind, your man, Ivan? She said no, Ivan was interested in wildlife documentaries and nature. He wasn't a gun person.

The credit card bills came, the bank statements, and she shoved them in the cupboard where the electric meter was. But they kept falling through the letterbox. She couldn't pay. She sold a lot of the stuff. There was a three-piece leather suite and it had to go. The woman who bought it only wanted one chair. That's why she still had that seat downstairs. Nobody would buy it. Now she had the problem of how to pay her debts. Buying stuff, Lee said, didn't bring you happiness. The great wisdom hung in the darkness. There was a man in the neighbourhood, connected, known, who could help people out with debt. When she spoke to him, he said he'd see what he could do. All he needed was a favour, and she thought that might mean working somewhere for a few nights. He had a social club. But he said, no love, just store something. My garage is full! he joked. A relief when he turned up and didn't have a van full of TVs, but then he went up into her roof-space. It took her a while but she found what he had put there. And now it was all she could ever think about. There was no sleep for her anymore because of the weight of the gun, up there. She could forget for a few moments but then it was there. In work the petrol pumps reminded her of it, the silver handle of the drawer, the cop who came in for a paper and a bag of crisps, she stared at his gun in the holster. Eileen, you got a thing for peelers? the guy that she worked with said after he'd left. She said yes, because she hoped that would explain it away. Did he not give you any idea, this man, Lee said, when he might return to pick it up? No, and he won't be back now because he's dead. Heart attack three months ago.

She couldn't just take it to the police. She would be prosecuted for having a weapon for all of these months. Lee suggested that maybe she could pretend that she just found it when she was out for a walk. Nice day, wanted to be out in the world of nature, maybe look at some birds, or see a squirrel, and then there it was, cold hunk of metal, over near some daffodils on the tow-path. That was no good either. She couldn't be sure that friends of the man wouldn't be back for the gun. Maybe other people knew about it. Probably. Possibly. And if she had given it to the police, what would they do to her?

Well, why didn't she bury the gun somewhere? That way it wouldn't be in her house. She wouldn't be thinking about it as much then. And if the guys came for it she could tell them where it was. Bury the gun!

Lee stared at the tangled cluster of tree air-fresheners hanging from the mirror. He was in Eileen's little old car at half five in the morning. The gun was in her handbag on the back seat, wrapped in two plastic bags. He asked where they were going and she said she didn't know. Somewhere with fields? he suggested. People were already standing at bus stops, their day already loading. He looked across at Eileen's pale face. Splits happened. Loads of bastards had hard times. If you decided that what you wanted to be was a pussy-assed motherfucker, letting others use you, then that was your problem. GABOS. Game ain't based on sympathy. Something flickered, his mother, on her own, him on the orange rug, playing with a toy, her on the sofa, making a noise into a cushion. Her face, when he got up and went over, her face wet as she tried to say with a smile, what'll we have for our tea? It flickered for a moment, and was gone. She was a supervisor now. That's what it said on her work badge. She was in charge of it all. He looked at Eileen again. GABOS, anyway.

You alright Eileen? he asked, as they headed out of the city along the motorway. It was beginning to get light now and the lough was not water but a grey slab, solid as concrete. They hit a roundabout and Lee pointed out the sign for a park. They had to take the roundabout again so that they could make the turn-off. When they parked the car, he looked quickly at the guy staring out beyond his windscreen at nothing. What was anyone doing here at this time of the morning? Eileen switched off the engine. So we're going to do it? he said. Yes, Eileen replied. What have you got in your boot? he asked. She said that she had a spare tyre. No, I mean, to dig with. She said she didn't have anything other than a jack. Well, Lee said, I don't think we can dig with a fucking jack. Would it be impossible for us to use our hands? Eileen asked.

They started down the path, Eileen with the handbag tucked under her arm. The birdsong was a racket. Even at home, where they were near fields, it didn't sound so insane. There was a massive tree, its trunk about a metre wide. Wouldn't you remember that place, Eileen? he said. It seemed a good spot and so they hunkered down to start clawing at the ground. They each kept looking around them, ready at any point to stand up straight and look as though the small hole was nothing to do with them. Scraping away the moss was fine, and the first few inches of soil, but beyond that they kept hitting hard roots, and so that spot had to be abandoned. They moved further away towards a configuration of bushes where the ground was softer, and wetter. They needed to dig deep because Eileen said, imagine if kids found it and one of them went into a school and shot people. The earth smelled like football boots. Keep going down, Eileen said and he replied, yeah, keep going, we are making progress. They got a rhythm going, his hands, and then her hands, scooping the dark soil. She put the strap of the bag across her chest so that she could work on the hole. A bell tinkled. Or maybe it was one of those birds. The sound got louder, louder, and then suddenly between them there was slavering brown muscle. Shakur! came the shout. Shakur. Studded lead in hand, a man, tough as his dog, stood above them. Good on ya, burying a body, he said. You need a hand? And now they did leap to their feet. What breed of dog is that? Eileen asked. Beautiful colour! We're digging, Lee explained, because just the other day we were here with the metal detector and it was going boogaloo at this spot. Beep beep beep. Thought there must be something down there. They said a loud no in unison when the guy asked them if they had found anything yet. Gotta keep searching, he said, before heading off with the dog. Now they had been seen, continuing was futile. They went back to the car, where Lee said there was also no point going back to the house. She dropped him off at the placement and as he got out of the car, he said that they would think of another plan.

Lee's a bit of a dark horse, Hendo said in the portacabin at lunch-time, after a morning spent loading boxes into vans. Yeah, said Tommy, we know what you've been up to. He thought of the birdsong ringing in his ears and the heat of that dog with the slobbering mouth. Yeah, bit of a dark horse. Saw you being left off this morning. That wasn't your ma, was it? He said that no, it was the woman he was staying with. The big guy said, maybe she's rich and you are the gold-digger. Not by the look of the car she was driving, Hendo replied. Looked like it should have been on the scrap heap. Maybe she just likes a good old seeing to by our boy here. He reached across to ruffle Lee's hair, roughly.

Bildungsroman

As he went round the whole of Warehouse 3, completing orders with an enormous shopping trolley, he thought about what else they could try. They could get up early the next day and find a better place to bury it, and bring a spade. If someone knew about the gun, they would have taken it by now. He had probably told no one, this guy who died of a heart attack. That's why no one had been back for it. This was the day when he should have been heading back home. But he was still at Eileen's.

Instead of taking his second bus, he walked out of the town back to Eileen's house. He took in the houses with the huge gardens and the sprinklers on the lawn, the flash cars in the driveways. He saw a woman, a nurse, or some kind of healthcare visitor, getting out of her car in her blue uniform. An old person was at the window, watching her walk up the drive. He thought about what he had seen on his phone. He had seen three beheadings. One of a woman being killed in a market place, and two with the guys in orange suits. He had seen the remains of a drug cartel execution in Mexico, hands lying in a deserted street. He thought of the muzzle of the gun cold at the base of his neck, the pressure that would send a bullet to his brain. It could lie in an attic, or it could be used. It could be used, or it could lie in an attic.

At the house, Eileen came to the door a little more quickly than usual, although still in the same beige tracksuit, and when they had their tea, she perched on a seat at the table for some of the time. She wanted to know, when they were sitting in the living room to watch the TV, if he had a new plan for what they should do. He said he had, and Eileen

121

leaned forward, from the strawberry leather, eager to hear. He looked at the stalks on the mantelpiece, wondering how to communicate it. Well, he said slowly, it's maybe not what you want to hear, but the thing is, it's safest with you. If this dead man's friends knew, they probably would have come for it by now. But let's hope they don't. It would be good, I suppose, if they came to get it, but bad too. Because as long as it stays with you, it can't do any harm. Before he played shooting games that took place in strip clubs and casinos, it was all about wizards and quests and magic tokens for him. He was reaching to resurrect a word from back then and it was custodian. So, he said, Eileen, you are the custodian of the gun. Because you have just got to put up with things. That's the best thing you can do. You have no choice. But it's good, to be the custodian of the gun.

On Lee's last day Hendo let him go an hour early. He even gave him a lift into town because he was heading to the hospital where his daughter had to be picked up from kidney dialysis. Before he left, he gave a slight wave in the direction of Tommy, who returned a slight nod. Best of luck, Lee said, although Tommy couldn't have heard it. Lee was leaving still knowing nothing about brand identity. That morning he had said goodbye to Eileen. Lee looked at her mouth, maybe a little less frayed at the edges, and wondered if he should give her a kiss, but decided against it. I'll be keeping in touch, he said, because she had given him her number.

The texts in answer to him were still coming back quickly, even three years after Lee's marriage split up. They were both too young. She said she didn't ever really love him, not really. She had met someone else who showed her what love really was. Lee had progressed to deputy manager of a phone shop. Then one time, there was no response. He messaged again the next week, phoned a few days later. Her brother didn't live next to his mother anymore; there was no place to make enquiries. When there was still no answer, he drove to Belfast. The hanging basket wasn't there anymore. The bell didn't work so he knocked on the pebbled glass, expecting that flesh-coloured movement, although surely, in all these years, she might have bought herself something new. He cupped his hands around his face as he peered into the living room window. And then he realised someone was watching him. She's passed away, the man said. Did you not know? We weren't at the funeral. We're just back from a holiday. He pointed at a touring caravan as proof. Lee asked what happened. A stroke, he thought, but he wasn't sure. It was all more blurred when Lee looked again at the dark shapes in the living room where he had last been nearly ten years ago.

He didn't think he would always work in the shop, but he wasn't sure what else he would do. He came in one evening after work, to the house he shared with three other guys, and found a letter that looked slightly ominous, the thickness of the paper, the way it had his full name. But it was from a woman called Anjali McClintock who, as the executor for E.G. Hughes, was kindly asking him to make an appointment. He didn't bother and another letter replied, more insistent, so on a Thursday afternoon, he made the drive to Belfast. Solicitor Anjali, it turned out, was an animated kind of person who looked as if, in the middle of the box files and rows of books, she'd do a high kick and burst into song. But it wasn't a musical. He was there to be told that he had been named in Eileen's will. It had taken them some time, Anjali said, to find him. There would be papers to sign in relation to what Ms Hughes had left him. He would have to come back again. But for now, she wanted to show him the details relating to what would soon be his. Lee saw that it was a house with a pink leather armchair and a handgun in the roof space.

Cell

Caro asks for a bread roll and a cup of tea. She is told, however, that the roll comes with the soup. But Caro doesn't want soup. She would just like one of the bread rolls and a cup of tea.

The thing is, the man says, the plain bread rolls are there to be had with the soup. Just the way we do it here.

She sighs. Even a place like this must apply arbitrary rules as an index of its authority.

Well, I suppose I'll just have the tea then, she says.

But the man brings over a bread roll anyway, plain with no butter.

The café is called Jack's American Diner. Propped on every table, next to the salt, pepper and red sauce, are little star-spangled banners. The menus resemble saloon doors.

When Caro goes to pay, she asks the man at the till why everything in the place is American.

What do you mean?

Why is everything American? she says, as she points at the looming Uncle Sam on the wall.

It is what it is, the man replies. American. American food. Isn't nearly everything American?

Caro considers this observation.

Yes, indeed, she says.

But I'll tell you what, love, if you don't like American, if you think that American is not for you, then there's the Wong Garden. The Wong Garden, you know, down the road, the Chinese?

Caro isn't interested in the Chinese. Of all the groups in their particular part of London, and there were many, those Maoists were the most risible, handing out their little samizdats in the market. Didn't they know that people only took them for a joke? She recalled Bill sticking them on the wall for everyone to ridicule.

Another thing, the man says. They might charge you for the prawn crackers. They won't be giving you a roll for nothing, love.

Time in the house accounted for almost a quarter of a century, and Caro's routine was usually to go to the shop in the morning. She would leave the house at precisely half-past eight because that gave sufficient time to prepare the breakfast for everyone. Each day she would purchase what was required for lunch and dinner, although she would buy whatever fruit was there on a Monday. Household products were reserved for the Friday trip when Luis might accompany her. Those sorts of provisions could be bulky. She and Luis didn't really speak; they had nothing to say to each other. Occasionally he nipped into a newsagent's where he knew the owner. On one occasion, Caro had suggested that it might perhaps be more economical to use a bigger supermarket just once a week but Bridget said, No way, you having a laugh? Well, are you? Having a laugh? Luis joined in, shaking his head. Having a laugh, you are.

There was of course much to recommend using the same small shop every day but at the beginning it felt limiting, with its particular selection of vegetables, although there were other things too, cereals and cleaning products, pot noodles. In the early days it was a man with glasses in the shop, or his wife. And then it was the new owner, new even when he'd been there at least a decade. Hello, good morning, he said, fine day! whether it was or wasn't. Caro used to supplement their provisions with what she managed to grow in the garden, but that depended on getting seeds. Bridget said on numerous occasions that she had sent off for them, but when they failed ever to arrive, Caro stopped asking about them.

In Belfast, she maintains a similar regimen in the mornings, except the shop is now Polish and there is no need to hurry back because no one other than herself requires breakfast. If she wished, she could go to the American diner every day in life for an American breakfast. The window of the Polish shop is partially concealed by an adhesive panel displaying close-ups of cheese and apples. Stuck around this are adverts for phone-cards. Stacks of plastic boxes sit outside, a makeshift display of potatoes, beetroot and some huge root vegetable she doesn't recognise. Inside she passes the deli counter with its hams and salamis to consider the astounding array of packets of soup. The pictures on the front may be wildly different, but she knows from experience that they all taste the same.

When the Polish government suppressed Solidarity and declared martial law, some people, such as Mark Mulgrew for instance, supported them. Bill had nearly punched him.

You are wrong on this, Bill said. Absolutely wrong. You'll look back, Mark, and you will know you were wrong.

In the shop it's always one of three girls who all wear tight jeans. The one with the red hair always forgets and greets Caro in Polish, but the other two don't say anything. She could spend five minutes in the shop, she could spend twenty. It doesn't really matter.

On the way to the shops she has to pass a hairdressing salon. Even if Caro takes her time, it's still the same women sitting in the same seats that she sees when she returns. The women with configurations of tinfoil folded into their hair are still reading the celebrity magazines. Caro hasn't been to a salon in decades because her own method has always been perfectly serviceable: grab a handful of hair at the right and cut whatever sticks out from your clenched fist, then do the same on the other side. The back she used to have to separate into two sections but now, because her hair has thinned, only one is required. Grab the back then snip. Admittedly the chop has a rough-hewn look for a few days, but with even a little wind and rain and general living it isn't long before this disappears. The technique blunts scissors, that's unavoidable, but new scissors every so often is still a relative economy. She used to have to ask Bridget to get new scissors. Bridget and Luis used clippers for their hair; Caro had to sweep up their cuttings from the kitchen floor. These days, she has started to use a balm on her lips but only because they were peeling and starting to bleed. The balm's use is medicinal rather than cosmetic. Personal titivation has never been a priority.

Caro wonders if today she will order a takeaway pizza. Her brother, when he brought her back, got her a phone and showed how to look things up on it. Caro searched for a range of people from the early days. Norman Patterson, she found out, is now the head teacher of a school in Liverpool, Sue Gregg is General Secretary of the British Airline Pilots Association, and Jimmy McCann, Professor of Social and Economic history in Glasgow. Mark Mulgrew runs a hotel in central France which gets a lot of five-star reviews. Judith Harkness handles PR for a mental health charity. There are others she can't find, and others she can't remember. She doesn't know exactly where Maurice is, but has no doubt he's being well looked after. Bill's long gone. Luis and Bridget have been separated.

Caro has got two apps on the phone. One is a game called Letter Soup where you are given six letters in a bowl of, unsurprisingly enough, soup, and you have to form the requisite number of words by drawing a line between the letters. There is a spoon you can use to stir the letters. It's possible to purchase hints but Caro doesn't bother because she can usually work it out eventually. She is now on Taste of Manila level. Next is Saigon Shack. She has also got a pizza delivery app which is quite something. She orders on the app and within half an hour the pizza comes. Caro orders the smallest pizza, which they call a 'personal pizza', but for delivery you have to spend more than that amounts to, which means she is obliged to order a side dish of something she doesn't necessarily want. She always makes a point of being very pleasant to the pizza delivery man when he arrives on his motorbike. Thanks. Thanks awfully.

Caro has tried to keep up with her reading. She works, as she has always done, with a pencil and notebook beside her. She has her own style of notation. But she just doesn't know what it is that makes reading so hard nowadays; she thought possibly it was just that she needed glasses, but the pair that she bought made no difference. She can't seem to concentrate, so understanding is only ever fleeting and she needs to read single sentences repeatedly before any meaning becomes apparent, or should she say meanings, because lots seem to crowd in. And these are books that she has read before many, many times, ones that she brought back from London with her. Voloshinov. Nikolai Marr. Books were really the only things in her suitcase. There is a magazine too that she reads, called *Take A Break*. She bought it once, enjoyed it very much, so now she gets it every week. The true-life stories are often quite shocking. A woman didn't know that her toyboy Latin lover was having sex with not only her daughter but also with her mother.

Belfast is a city but it isn't a city, not really. In either direction from her living room Caro can see hills, dense green against grey roofs. So much space: by the flats there's a grassy area with benches, and even between the shops there are some empty squares of scrub, plastic bags caught on the thistles. The goal posts of the school rugby field peek over the tops of the houses. But this is where Caro now lives, a one-bedroom flat which her brother found, a flat near a roundabout. He sends her messages on the phone. All okay? Yes, thank you very much, she replies. He has invited her to his place to spend Christmas with his wife and daughter. Christmas? She hasn't celebrated it in decades. His daughter has come round a couple of times. She has a pierced lip which always looks swollen. The first time she appeared it was on a Tuesday. Caro remembers this because that's the day *Take a Break* comes out and she had it in her bag ready to read. The girl had said, Hi Auntie Caroline, do you know who I am? Caro wanted to read her magazine.

In London, it had always been important to get back from the shop because there was such a lot to do. Everything had to be done, as they say, from scratch. Granted, Luis liked pot noodles if he was on the move, but everything else required preparation. She had to bake bread every day. All washing was done by hand. At one point a washer-drier did arrive—yes, it was quite thrilling when that came. Caro read the instruction booklet carefully but the multiplicity of options was almost overwhelming; there didn't seem to be any eventuality that the machine couldn't cope with. She could even take down the curtains in all of the rooms and wash them. It wasn't impossible to do that by hand, but it would have been difficult to get them dry. Incredible that the same machine could both wash and dry. Maurice, it has to be said, had very few clothes. If they needed to be washed, she had to put a blanket round him until they were ready to be put on again. Sometimes this took quite a while.

Why even bother? Bridget said. Sure they'll be dirty again within a couple of hours! Let him stay in them.

Luis had allergies which meant he had to get new bedding quite frequently; Bridget bought it somewhere. That washer-drier was left by the delivery people at the front of the house and Caro moved it to the kitchen, laboriously inching it down the hallway. But then they didn't know anyone to plumb it in.

Can't you do it, Caro? Is that not your department? Bridget said. Haven't you read the instructions? Christ Almighty, can you not get it sorted?

Caro looked again but the instructions for plumbing it in said, more or less, to get a plumber. If it had been in one of the squats there would have been no difficulty getting a plumber because in the squats there were always people able to do whatever was required, but in this instance they needed to find an actual plumber. Bridget hadn't wanted to do that.

We wouldn't know who they are, she said. They could be anyone. We can't risk it. It's our involvement in things, see. We've managed up to this point without one of these machines.

And so it just sat there, pristine and un-plumbed in. After a while things got placed on top of it. The drum was used to store fruit.

At intervals, other items arrived. There was a toasted sandwich maker, and an ice-cream machine. Bridget and Luis loved ice-cream for a while. Plus, it stopped you getting osteoporosis. Caro thought that it was perhaps a food that Maurice could eat, since it slipped down easily, but he didn't care much for it. It melted back to nothing in his room. For a few weeks Caro was mainly responsible for the sales of double cream in the shop. The appetite eventually waned for ice-cream and the machine sat redundant by the fridge. The Ramoska, which was a mini-cooker from somewhere in eastern Europe. Caro liked the utilitarian simplicity of the Ramoska. They were still using the Ramoska right up until the point when everything collapsed. And the fan heaters made a significant difference: they were a welcome arrival. The central heating in the house rarely worked; there were elaborate clangs and gurgles when it was switched on, but the actual result was only tepid metal in the lower parts of the radiators.

They need to be bled! Bridget had said, looking at Caro. There's nothing actually wrong with them, that's all you need to do.

But Caro didn't know how to bleed a radiator.

You need some kind of a key, Bridget said, as though all would be easy if only they had this implement. Caro wished she knew how to do it but she didn't. Did Luis know?

Luis's a painter and decorator, Bridget said.

Yeah, said Luis. Painter and decorator.

But then the fan heaters arrived. It was remarkable the difference they made to the house, the enveloping warmth which put everyone in a more favourable mood. She remembered that when the fan heaters arrived, they sat at the kitchen table and had a pot of tea and toast. She had brought Maurice's up to him, cut up into fingers, put on the plate in a criss-cross. The fan heaters were however only for use downstairs. It was an extreme fire hazard to have something like that in a bedroom. Bridget was convinced of that.

*

You didn't work, did you? one of the people asked her, when they were doing their investigation. You didn't work, did you? Which one of them asked her that, when she sat in the interview room: the thin man who fired questions in a monotone, the black woman who wore a cross that she kept touching, the plangent young fellow, the throaty blonde woman, the one who thought he was a comedian, the angry man. They carried files and notebooks and tape-recorders. What a question to ask! She never stopped working! Not a prisoner, you say, so when did you leave the house? When did Maurice leave the house, before that evening? When had he last left the house? Anyway, those interrogators had a definition of work that was predictably narrow, their interest purely in institutional classification. First-class honours degree, it says here, you got a first-class honours degree? Says here you did two years of post-grad work, and then you worked, where was it, a library? Yeah, says here a library. And then—that was it, end of the line for you, as far as work was concerned?

When the library closed she had in fact got another job—as a research assistant, albeit only very briefly. She remembered the interview and how the panel of three women nodded as she spoke. She hadn't heard herself say so much in a long time. When the letter came to say that she had been successful, Bridget said that she was unsure of the organisation.

I've never heard of them. I've asked around and no one seems to have heard of them. You need to be one hundred per cent sure about who you are working for, you know what I mean, Caro? One hundred per cent.

True, it was a group that Caro had not heard of before either but she imagined that it would broadly be in line with their views. Bridget asked how much Caro would be earning.

Phew, she said. You'll be living the high life! You're a fucking yuppie cunt.

But the wage was modest enough really. Caro did wonder if she had made a mistake when on the first day so many people were introducing themselves; she had been used to a solitary existence in the library, cataloguing and filing, but here they all asked questions. Caro hadn't expected that the personnel of a child poverty charity would be quite so effervescent, so possibly Bridget was right to have her doubts. At the end of the week Caro was obliged to go for a drink after work. People sat around talking about their marital problems and their sex lives and their children and what plans they had for the weekend. One person was doing a sky dive. A recently bereaved woman told everyone about how she and her boyfriend were trying to clear out her mother's house, but so much of what they were coming across ended up making her cry. It was only a fucking mug! the woman said. Only her fucking yellow mug and I was in pieces! Could hardly pull myself together! Caro watched another woman give her a hug. What you need, this woman said, is another drink. Or two. Caro said nothing. She had not been in contact with her own mother for a number of years. Visits home had dwindled to nothing. She hadn't even bothered opening the occasional letters that came with a Belfast postmark.

They wouldn't even know her address now. She supposed she had, in effect, disowned them.

When she returned to the house that evening and Bridget heard where she had been, she said, Oh very social of you. You drinking martinis? Oh Caro, this is the new you. Did you tell them that Daddy's a fucking judge? Bet they loved that!

On the Monday when Caro came home there was a puppy in the hall that had just produced a squirt of diarrhoea. Couldn't resist him, Bridget said. He's called Patrick. I need to go out now. Luis won't be back till late.

Luis, too, disapproved of the new job.

This food, he said, it tastes, not right. I don't like the food. And he pushed away his plate. It was true that she had burnt the dhal that she was making, something that she never did, and it was inconvenient for the others to have to do the shopping. The library job had not started until later, whereas with this new one she had to leave the house at seven o'clock to get there on time. And then there was Maurice: Bridget and Luis said that during the day it was impossible for them to devote time to Maurice. Luis's painting and decorating was on and off, that was the way things worked in that kind of trade, but that didn't mean he could commit to checking in on Maurice.

We really rely on you, Caro, to support what we're involved with, Bridget said. And so within four weeks Caro left the job. They wanted to go for a drink to say goodbye but she had said no, she couldn't, she was terribly sorry. They gave her a card signed by a few people. All the best of luck! Very best wishes! The person who had been the runner-up at the interview was due to start the week after. Bridget decided that in fact Patrick was too difficult for them to manage and she was unsure of its temperament so the dog was given away to someone that Luis knew.

Back in time, when Caro was at school, there was a shabby hotel that specialised in under-age discos. Under a dusty disco-ball were the sons and daughters of almost every doctor and solicitor in that part of the city. Caro went once but did not enjoy it. It was astounding how other people could move so fluidly, how they were able to discern a beat which she couldn't hear. Her clothes weren't tight enough; she felt encumbered by bunches of fabric. The seats in the dark disco were curved velour plush and Caro found one at the very back that was beside a radiator. She ran her hand up and down its warmth but when the slow dances started, she went to the toilets.

It took only one small thing to nudge someone towards attractiveness: the curve of a thigh or a breast, the arc of a cheek. But Caro knew she looked like a hare. Her face was bony and her eyes bulged. Those other girls dancing at the disco, the supposed sophisticates, were in fact content to stay put and become university students who ate every night at the family dinner table and who slept in childhood beds still weighed down by cuddly toys. Are you sure? the people in the school said to Caro when she expressed her intention to go to UCL to study linguistics. Yes, thank you. Quite sure. Thank you very much.

That first term was a terrible disappointment, but to say that, she thought, suggested it was the place's fault when in fact it was her, and her lack of whatever it was. The course was interesting enough, but a city seen on television and in films was still something she just looked at. Caro, listening to others' conversations, was always surprised by their banality, yet could think herself of nothing to say. She invested in new clothes, a black jumper and short black skirt, because she had seen someone wear something similar and thought it stylish. The colour drained her so she chose a hard red lipstick that she dragged across her mouth. Mortifying that she was now homesick for a place she had never liked in the first instance, thinking fondly of the disco and the roadworks that she used to pass every day on her way to school, the flutter of the cordon tape in the wind.

Friends were having a party, someone in the group outside the lecture theatre said. Just a house party, but all welcome if they fancied it. He gave the address. If anyone was surprised to see Caro turn up in the black jumper and mini skirt and the red lipstick they didn't say so. She got very drunk very quickly on a concoction that had been made in a bread bin and splashed into glasses with a plastic ladle. There were lamps with scarves draped over them, stripped mattresses for seats. Caro sank into one of them and wondered if she would ever be able to get up again. A flow of indeterminate sound passed by as she looked for a familiar face somewhere, anywhere, but then there was a hand on her leg, fingers splayed, followed soon after by a mouthful of liver-like tongue. Lucid through the colossal effort of trying not to be sick, Caro thought, so, so, this is a party, this is you, this is you at a party, being a young person and doing the things that young people do.

And then a hand was kneading her left breast. It stopped suddenly when another person sat down.

When Caro came home that Christmas there was a knock at the door of her bedroom one night and it was her mother. You know, her mother said, if you find it difficult, you can come home again. No one would think any the less of you.

But Caro continued to work at her desk. I don't really know what you mean, she said.

Well, if you say so, her mother said. She closed the door again.

The next term, Caro went along to a talk at the students union after a young man had handed her a flyer in the street. Why not go? she had thought. The small crowd of mostly post-grad students waited patiently in the hall for half an hour before someone came along to say the event had been cancelled. The young man who had given her the flyer was there. He was apologetic. He knew the speaker, he said, and could only imagine he must have had very good reason to cancel like that. The young man intended to meet some friends later on—would she want to come too? These friends would likely be of interest, if she had been prepared to hear the speaker. He and Caro walked for what seemed like an hour and a half to arrive at a second-floor flat. The young man said his name was Bill. There were fifteen or twenty people crammed in the main room and from the bare lightbulb overhead hung an illuminated triangle of smoke. Bill! somebody shouted. Listen to this! You're not going to believe it!

And who are you? a woman asked.

Sue, this is a friend of mine, Bill said. This is Caroline.

Sue said nothing but shook her hand.

Car – o – line, the woman at Sue's side said. Caro. What can you do, Caro?

I don't know, she said.

And this is Bridget, Bill said, of the woman at Sue's side.

Maurice had been there too, his hair thin even then and fluffy, honey coloured. He picked at the fraying edge of his jumper; he was always doing that, picking at things, dry skin, loose threads. It was always the same way with Maurice. Disagreeing but too nervous to speak, he would tip his head to one side and stare up at the ceiling but then later, once the conversation had moved on to an entirely different topic, he would articulate with quiet elegance what was wrong with the previous analysis. By then, however, it would be too late and everyone would just find him an irritation. That was Maurice and he should have spoken up at the right time.

Bridget wasn't fat then, although she was, later on. It was her right to be fat, if she wanted. Fat Cat, they called her in the paper. Incredible Bulk. It was only because by contrast Maurice was so thin. The brainwashed Belfast boffin. Jailbreak. They had a picture of Bridget in a wheelchair. That was how she arrived at court, wearing a dress with pleats that fanned out across the width of the chair. In the photo she was clutching a patent handbag. Bridget with a handbag! The paper was lying on the table in the hostel. Nobody living there cared particularly; they all had their own considerations.

Caro had started to visit that flat every week. There were

speakers, demos, papers, house resolutions, discussions and debates and at times anger. But there was also a sense of optimism and imminence. Caro listened to the projections of Bill and the others; she heard Mark Mulgrew bat away a newcomer who was reaching for unnecessary specifics. I can't put a date on revolution! he said. Caro was now greeted by name; everyone knew she'd done the reading and that she knew the arguments. Perhaps she was still a little uneasy when discussion turned to the Irish question because she saw her elegant tree-lined road, her double-fronted house. But it was obvious: divisions among the people were the result of false consciousness which was the consequence of imperialism.

The university course receded in importance. Some on her floor in Ramsey Halls had a party for an international student's birthday. They talked about revision schedules and where they were hoping to go for the summer, the lightness of the sponge of the birthday cake, which of the medical students they thought the most handsome. You're not saying much, Caroline, one of them remarked. I don't have much to say, she said. Well, she didn't have much to say about cake.

On the road there is a shop that sells material and it is one of Caro's favourite places to go. Garish, clashing, gorgeous bolts of stuff are stacked on all sides. The colours are exciting. Spools of thread are laid out in the colours of the prism, so many gradations that the point of change from red to orange, from orange to yellow is imperceptible. Caro likes to stare at them, trace the colours through and then back again. The first time she did that the man had asked her if there was anything that she wanted.

Oh no, I'm fine, thank you, she said. It's just lovely to look at the threads. The colours.

Well, tell you what, you should've seen what the place used to be like, he said. This place is a shadow of its former self.

Caro looked around. That's hard to imagine, she said.

Yeah. Well. It's nothing compared to what we used to have here. We used to have Harris Tweed, we used to have Liberty prints, we used to have Moygashel, heavy silks, satins, really good velvets. Oh yeah. Shop would have been coming down with the stuff. Too much nearly. Hardly a garment factory in the whole of the UK now, decline of British manufacturing, because what we have here, these bolts, are offcuts. Seem big in here but they're only factory offcuts. No factories anymore means nothing for us. I think that what we need in this country is more entrepreneurs.

Caro looked at the shimmering bolts of hot pink froth.

I think what we need is more British manufacturing and more entrepreneurs in this country, he said. Are you wanting to buy anything, sweetheart?

She picked at random a spool from the display, a royal blue, in isolation unimpressive.

The very first place on Railton Road had been a good spot to live, despite there being no central heating and no water for much of the time. Above them was a press that published assorted pamphlets, you could hear them working through the night, and on the ground floor there was a volunteer café. Always a stream of people passing through. Everyone knew not to ask too many questions. There was one man with a Belfast accent who, when he heard Caro speak, asked her where she was from. Belfast, same as you, she said. But where in Belfast? he said. Where? There was the runaway from Glasgow in denim shorts who someone had let stay for a couple of nights. She spoke to Caro later on in the night when the others had gone to bed and as she talked she painted her nails. Yiz are away with the fairies, she said. Is that so? Caro said. It is so, she said. Don't like the big queen bee. And her sleazy wee fancy man can get to fuck. Bridget and Luis are revered comrades, Caro said. The girl shrugged and carried on painting her nails.

Love was merely a construct, monogamy a means of social control. Luis and Bridget were married, it was said, but that seemed only to ensure Luis's residence. Bill and Maurice, that was different. Caro knew a woman who lived in a household with six mothers and fourteen children, each of whom had no more attachment to one mother over another. The children had no toys or clothes of their own: everything was one communal pile.

There were so many other places where they lived in the early years, various configurations of men and women, grouping, falling apart, re-grouping. Some embraced alternative ideologies. John Leahy-Simpson took a sabbatical from his medical course and went to Kenya where he became a Christian. Norman Patterson went all gooey over a woman with long black hair who was one of the Aleister Crowley acolytes and so he moved in with them. Another person joined the primal screamers. Caro remembered when the primal scream group decamped to Sligo, or was it Donegal? Somewhere in the middle of nowhere anyway, where they could continue their shrieking without any hassle.

Caro came home to Belfast for two weeks during the first summer. She had envisaged long and combative discussions over the dinner table, but everyone in the house was absorbed in their own pursuits. Her mother met endless friends for coffee or lunch, and devoted the rest of her time to sporting activities. Caro's father left early in the morning and did not return until late at night. Her thirteen-year-old brother spent most of his time hitting a ball against the side of the house. She tried to talk to him about contemporary issues. Right, I see, he said. But do you? Caro asked. Not really, he admitted.

Her mother played golf in the morning and tennis in the afternoon. You want to join me, Caroline? You used to be good at tennis, she said.

Why don't you take him? Caro said, pointing at her brother.

He needs more lessons.

Her father asked her where she was going to be living when she started back for the next year.

I'll be living, Caro said, in a squat in Brixton.

Well that will save me some money anyway. His voice shaded into professional dryness. There are limits, however, Caroline. As to how you can conduct yourself. I'm sure you understand.

Her brother said he wouldn't mind going to the funfair

at the King's Hall. It was only going to be there for another couple of days. You sure you want to go with me? Caro asked. You'd not rather go with some friends? They were there early in the morning and it was empty, no queues, and the bright, brassy music bounced off the walls. They gave the ghost train a miss. The fluorescent spectres looked tired and the witch at the entrance waved her arm not very menacingly. You got any change, Caroline? he asked. I wouldn't mind a go on that over there. So they went to the rifle range which was decked out in camouflage and which featured on the surround what looked like angry members of the Vietcong. Her brother took aim and hit one wooden barrel out of five.

They went to the café where they shared a plate of chips.

When you going back again? he asked.

In a few days.

Right, he said. It's just I thought you might be staying longer.

No, I need to get back.

What for?

Just do.

Maybe I could come and visit you, he said.

Caro shrugged. Maybe.

She was looking forward to getting back.

What you going to do for the rest of the summer? she asked him.

Don't know. Nothing much.

He took a drink of his Coke.

You think there's going to be a nuclear war before too long?

I hope not.

Yeah, me neither.

He took another swig of his drink.

So are you and your friends basically trying to change the entire world? he asked.

Not really, Caro said. Well I suppose so, kind of.

Could you start by blowing up my school?

Caro laughed. Do you not like school, then?

No, he said. I can't stand it. Can't stand anything about it. Teachers. Other kids. Hate it all.

It might get better.

Yeah, he said. Oh well, doesn't matter.

On the bus back home, they sat facing empty seats and her brother put his feet up on them. A fellow passenger said, Would you mind taking your feet off the seats, please, son?

Her brother said sorry, and took his feet away. Sorry, he said again, when his feet were firmly planted on the floor of the bus.

And why's it any concern of yours? Caro asked the man.

It's the rules. You don't put your feet up on the seats.

Do you work for Citybus?

I don't, but it's the rules.

Rules, rules, rules, Caro said to her brother. Fascist.

What did you say? the man asked.

Nothing.

Could you believe him? her brother said when they were off the bus. What a fascist.

The council was knocking down buildings and the whole Railton Road scene felt precarious when the possibility of the house in north London presented itself. There would be a nucleus of Maurice, Bill, Bridget, Luis and Caro. The house was something different. With its sitting room and fire place and neat kitchen, it seemed like a set from an old-fashioned play. There were three bedrooms and a fully functioning bathroom. There wasn't a lock on the toilet. There wasn't a lock on Maurice's door. Luis and Bridget took the largest bedroom and although Caro would have taken the smallest one, Bill said that he and Maurice would have it.

But Bill, lovely Bill was in an accident only a few months after they all moved in, hit by a bus when cycling back from somewhere or other. Caro came back from the library to find Luis and Bridget silent in the kitchen and Maurice upstairs.

It didn't really work without Bill.

They went to the place where Bill had grown up, about ten of them. They saw the two younger brothers in stiff clothes and the white-faced mother and father. The mother couldn't speak to anyone outside the church. Caro and Sue Gregg shook the father's hand, but Maurice stood by himself over near the gate. No one went into the church to hear the minister, but when proceedings moved to the graveyard they formed part of the circle looking down at the coffin. Then Jimmy McCann produced a ghetto-blaster from the plastic bag he had been carrying, pressed play, and across the graveyard rang the sound of The Internationale. It drowned out the minister and whatever it was he was saying. One of the relatives came up to Jimmy McCann when they were leaving the cemetery. I hope you bastards are proud of yourselves, he said. Oh yeah, Jimmy replied. We are.

In her Belfast flat, Caro's door is white PVC, substantial enough perhaps, but the pebbled windows allow someone to peer in quite effectively if they put their face close enough to the glass. That's what the niece did when she came again. Caro would rather have something solid, formidable, painted black. The niece rang the bell, which Caro ignored, but she stood outside waiting to see some movement. Caro edged down the hall towards the bathroom, but then Hi! Aunt Caroline!

Sorry, Caro said when she opened the door, I was asleep.

She wondered if she should buy black paper to stick over the glass.

Well, her niece said, I have just had, like, the biggest fight ever with Dad. You won't believe it. Shit went down. And I mean, down.

Caro made a cup of tea while the niece relayed through to the kitchen a three-way argument between her, her mother and her father. And then she says and then he says and then I say and then they say and then I say—So what you think of that then? It sounded exhausting. What had started as an argument over who would give her a lift to a friend's house seemed to have become monumental. They hated everything about her, her parents, particularly this. Particularly what? The niece had pulled up her sleeve. This, she said. There was a miniscule tattoo of a music note. It was actually illegal, you know, to get it done, her niece said, because I'm under eighteen. But the tattoo guy thought I was over eighteen so that was pretty good.

Well I'm sure that you can resolve matters, Caro said. None of it seems insurmountable.

I suppose.

Yes, said Caro. These things, I'm sure they'll pass. The situation will return to normal.

Normal, the niece said. Who wants to be normal?

The niece asked about London. How long was she there for? Why did she come back? What was it like, living in London? The niece had been on a school trip to London; she listed all the places she had visited, going back to the start of the list every time she added somewhere new. Some girls had been suspended because they'd been drinking in the rooms of the hotel and they'd had random boys back. She hadn't been involved in that though.

I would ask you to stay for something to eat, said Caro, but I don't have anything in.

I'll call in another day, the niece said.

Certainly, replies Caro.

She watches the girl cross the road and wonders what age she is. Fifteen, sixteen?

Caro doesn't care too much about cooking for herself and a loaf of bread lasts a week. In the Railton Road days she got quite skilled at cooking for large numbers. (In the house, although there was only a few of them, Bridget and Luis were very exacting in their requirements.) There is a community centre only five minutes' walk from Caro's flat. She walked past it numerous times before taking the audacious step of entering. Even now she is surprised that she did it. There was a warren of rooms suitable for meetings and discussions but activity primarily seemed to be sports-based, with football being played both inside and out. Caro found herself in the big kitchen, industrial stainless steel, it smelt of burnt toast and bleach.

Can I help you? a woman said. You looking for somebody?

No. I was just thinking, what a beautiful kitchen. I was in a hostel for a while and the kitchen in the hostel was a little like this. Possibly not quite as large.

The woman who had a whistle round her neck stared at her.

I suppose I thought, well, perhaps I could get involved here.

Involved in what, love?

Involved in whatever it is you're doing.

We've got a kids' tournament later on in the week, if you're any use at refereeing.

Well, I would have no experience in that kind of thing at all.

I was joking, love, the woman said. It's okay.

Everyone liked Bill, but Maurice was the only one who loved him. After Bill's death, Maurice stayed in his room for much of the time. The interrogators asked, In all that time from when the guy died, you never noticed he was getting ill, you never noticed any deterioration? Come on now, come on, Caroline. Really? You never noticed how unwell he was? Plus, you went into his room but you never went into Bridget and Luis's? Really? How could that be the case? The man who spoke in a monotone posed these questions. All that time, how could that be the case? It had always been made clear that she wasn't to enter Bridget and Luis's room: she didn't question it because she had no reason to. Caro heard them sometimes, laughing, and there were times when, if they had fallen out, they threw things. Yes, she knew they had a television, it wasn't a secret, she could hear it sometimes. They needed a television for the things that they needed to monitor. The woman with the cross had asked if she thought that Bridget had suffered domestic abuse at the hands of Luis. So many women were vulnerable. So many women were manipulated, the woman with the cross had said. She had seen it over and over again, she said. Luis? Abuse Bridget? Absolutely not. Don't be so ridiculous. But what about you, Caroline? the woman asked. What about you? Were you sexually assaulted by Luis?

Of course she hadn't been sexually assaulted by Luis. One time Bridget asked Caro if she thought Luis was attractive. Did she? She'd probably lived in the house with him for a year at this point but she hadn't, she had to admit, ever given it too much consideration. Luis was just always there. Always eating. Always lying on the sofa. Always in the toilet for a long time. Oh, come on, Caro, Bridget said. You know I'm not going to care what you say. We've moved beyond that and we moved beyond it a long time ago. Luis tells me about all of those bored little housewives that he fucks while their wankstain husbands are away slogging their guts out, bitches glamming themselves up to sit on their own sofas. But Luis tells me all the details, know what I mean, painting and decorating, yeah yeah yeah, no it's all that smooth skin buffed down the salon, all those bodies plumped by fancy restaurant food being fucked senseless by our very own little geezer, Bridget laughed. Oh yeah, I get all the details.

And she paused as if to consider them again.

But anyway, Caro, the thing is, Bridget continued, Luis finds you very attractive. He does. I'm just letting you know.

Caro didn't know what to say. It seemed preposterous. She couldn't think of a situation in which she could have appeared attractive. Doing the dishes? Going up the stairs? It was a novelty to be considered attractive. So feel free, Bridget said. Be my guest.

Thanks.

Unless, said Bridget, you are holding out for some handsome young man to come along and whisk you away to a lovely little semi somewhere. Been holding hands in the cinema with someone? Oh my god, he's just put his hand on your knee, what a bad boy. Stop it, bad boy, stop it!

Luis hadn't shown any more interest in her than usual the next day when Caro put his food in front of him at breakfast. Yet when she crossed her legs she thought these are the legs of an attractive person and they did look a little different, taut rather than knock-kneed. Her chin tilted upwards. Her neck lengthened.

In bed she read her book with unusual concentration, pausing at the end of each paragraph to make her notes. There was the noise of hot-water pipes and she could sense the others still padding around, Bridget's heavy footsteps on the stairs. She read a while longer but when she eventually put down the book she didn't switch off the bedside light. She lay there waiting, staring at the plasterwork which was more ornate than she had ever really noticed before. Just as she was wondering if nothing would actually happen, the door slid open and Luis was standing there. He was in a white dressing gown that said Slaley Court Hotel in black embroidery. Caro knew she could probably have said to him, What in god's name are you doing? and he would have slipped away again just as silently and the door would have closed behind him. But she said nothing and he advanced towards the bed. She took off her T-shirt and pulled off her old pyjama bottoms, their cartoon characters faded to outlines. She became interested in folding them very precisely, vertically and then horizontally. Luis undid the tie of the dressing gown. He looked as though she should be impressed. What? she said. She looked at his penis and back up to his face. What? He was stroking it in the absorbed, unhurried way she remembered people petting the guinea pigs that were brought to her primary school one day. And then it started. She focused on the bedside light which was an anglepoise one. The metal arm looked very much like the shower attachment in the bathroom, something she hadn't noticed before. But what was necessary was to marshal her thoughts so that she could appreciate the significance of what was occurring.

It happened again a couple of days later, but it was more rushed, and then a further three times during a six-month period after that. It was neither enjoyable nor unenjoyable. On one occasion Luis was very drunk and he called her baby. Come on, baby. Okay, baby. That's it, baby. Wider, baby. What's that you're saying? Caro asked. Luis said it again, mumbled it, and then after that kept quiet. The whole thing could hardly have furnished Bridget with much interesting detail; it was probably disappointing for her in that respect. Strange afterwards to walk past Luis in the hall or have him beside her on the way to the shops: she could almost believe she had imagined the whole episode.

In the early days of the house, after the initial stages of grief, Maurice did still go out. He liked long walks. He got buses to places. He told Caro he'd been back to the grave and that he'd stayed there all day even though the rain never stopped. He was in his room a lot too, listening to the World Service most of the night. He slept a lot during the day. Caro would leave food for him in the fridge and she would find it gone at some point. Occasionally she went with him on his walks. Even now, when out and about, she sometimes gives some thought to what Maurice might find interesting, were he there. If Maurice chose to talk, he did so with colons, semicolons, parentheticals. She and Maurice might have stopped for a while in a cafe, but it got so that he shook and his hands couldn't hold a cup of tea. When he saw that he was spilling it everywhere, the motion became a swing. Sometimes he could cry in the street. It would frighten people and they would stare accusingly at Caro. Why bring this out onto the pavement, we don't want to see this!

Mostly Maurice, back when they did actually go out, kept by her side. Over time he grew frightened of traffic, the hiss of a bus's hydraulic brakes or the swipe of a car's stereo. There were occasions when he got lost. The final straw was in a big department store.

But what were you even doing in there? Bridget shrieked when told.

It had been raining and they needed somewhere to go. Caro despised the sweeping staircase and the glittering counters and the shining floors, of course. She couldn't find Maurice anywhere. After forty minutes of going round men's jackets, the homeware basement, the make-up counters, the lifts, the toilets, the stairwells, she was frantic. Bridget would be furious. The shop might have found him and called the police. But Maurice was in ladies' fashions, staring at some cashmere jumpers. Caro shouldn't have mentioned it to Bridget because she got so agitated. But she just wanted to explain why they had been away for so long.

That's it, Bridget said, you are going to need to stay local. That's if he goes out at all. Meant to be very wet over the next couple of weeks. Maybe just stay in. We don't want him catching his death of cold.

In the house they all took Berocca, Maurice included. Luis had a friend who guaranteed it would prevent illness of all kinds and this friend got them huge amounts of Berocca at a much reduced price. They took triple the recommended daily amount, but mixed it with milk, not water. Luis said this released something extra in the drink. Nowadays, Caro sees the Berocca on the shelf when she goes to the chemist's shop, the green and yellow packets. She was surprised to note that it comes in different flavours and could be taken in tablet form too. Sometimes she thinks about buying it. She takes it from the shelf but puts it back again.

When the interrogators were talking to her, there were the polystyrene cups and Caro bit round the edge of them, little necklaces of teeth marks. She has the cups now in the flat and there are at least two shops on the road where they are available. She keeps them next to the microwave her brother got her. She was glad to see them in the shops: always those cups, whoever it was in front of her. She grew accustomed to them.

Luis and Bridget sometimes went away, just for the night. They didn't offer any explanation as to where they were going and Caro didn't ask. Have to go away again, Bridget said; it seemed something of an ordeal. Caro didn't know what they were or weren't involved in, and no, she didn't ask. You just didn't. Somewhat in the dark then, Caroline, the throaty blonde woman commented. Somewhat in the dark about the world outside. You never read a paper, Caroline? No? 9/11? Don't tell me you never heard of 9/11? People living in mud huts heard of 9/11. Of course she had heard of 9/11. Maybe you thought Maurice was involved and that's why he had to be kept prisoner. That right, Caroline? You thought Maurice was public enemy number one?

One morning on the way to the shop Caro saw a poster about a protest against the conversion of local council housing into offices. When she got home she wrote the date, time and place in her notebook. She went back and read her notes numerous times during the day. She needed to broach the subject with Bridget. She would like to go. It had been so long since she had done anything, got involved in anything, and the time had come, the time had come. It was different for Bridget and Luis. They were active. But Bridget crumpled the flyer into a ball.

It's not that I disagree on principle, I suppose, but you're wanting to support the local council. You're wanting to support the local authority. That seems, well, Caro, it seems weird.

No, it's the idea of council housing I'm supporting, it's not the council.

But you don't live in a council house. Strange you've never been in council housing all these years but council housing is your new big thing, huh?

Caro didn't go. Three o'clock would have been her new big thing. She couldn't remember the last time she had been out of the house at three o'clock.

On the night it happened, Bridget and Luis were away. They had left with a small suitcase. Caro noticed the whiteness of Luis's new trainers. Maurice had not eaten anything that day or the day before. When she went up to the bedroom, the plate was untouched. Caro hadn't been absolutely certain about the bucket idea and although she tried to empty it as frequently as possible, the smell lingered. That window only opened about six inches. Was the toilet so very far away, only down the hall?

Well, said Bridget, you can make him go to the toilet if you want to, but he'll need to have you around. Embarrassing for him really. Kinder just to do it this way. But if you can't hack the slopping out.

Oh, I can, Caro said.

Yeah, well, Bridget said, dunno if it sounds like it.

Maurice was making a noise that she hadn't heard before, a repetitive wheeze. Green bile was over his bed clothes so Caro took the quilt from the tent in her room to swap with Maurice's. She would wash it later when she got the chance. Maurice, she said, I'm changing your bedding. Maurice. But there was no response. His face looked crumpled. Maurice, stop that! Caro didn't know what to do. Maurice, she said. Maurice! Come on, now. Come on. But only that wheeze, rattle and wheeze. She needed to speak to someone about this but she didn't know how to contact Bridget and Luis. She didn't know where they were and there was no phone in the house. Luis had a mobile phone but she didn't know the number. Maurice was still breathing and that was something. Maurice, she said. Please say something. There were the neighbours. But they didn't speak to the neighbours. They didn't like them. Young men in their twenties, already in suits. They got pizzas delivered but they'd come not just once but twice to the wrong house. The second time Bridget had gone downstairs, taken the pizza and hurled it across the road. From the window Caro saw the pizza man pick it up. Bridget had gone over, pulled it out of his hand and thrown it away again.

It didn't seem possible to ask the neighbours what to do. There was 999, she remembered that, but without a phone what was the point of 999? Perhaps Bridget and Luis might be back soon anyway. She should wait. She knew they had a suitcase with them, but something might have happened to make them come back early. She went up again to look at Maurice who was now a terrible colour, so really there was nothing for it but she would have to go next door to ask to use their phone. But when she went out, she always turned left to go to the shop—she didn't turn right. She didn't turn right to go next door. She turned left.

She should have put on a coat because it was cold wearing only pyjama bottoms and a T-shirt. The darkness outside lapped against her as she passed the metal shutters of closed shops, looked up at yellow street-lamps. She could see a phone box on the other side of the road. Caro hesitated crossing and the green man looked impatient with her, that bend of his arms, his efficient pointy little feet, indicating move! move!

The handle felt heavy in her hand, but the woman had a warm voice. Say that again for me, would you? Let me repeat that back to you. Caro was in fact sorry when the phone call was over and she had to make her way back to the house again. She almost thought that the dark could dye her, but still her hands gleamed white when she raised them up to her face.

When the two men arrived, they followed her up to Maurice's room.

What's his name, love? You his wife?

Maurice Harrison.

Strange to say that full name when he had just been Maurice for so long.

They wanted to know if he was on any medication.

Oh no, Caro had said. I don't think so. He takes Berocca. We all take Berocca.

Uh huh, the man said. Berocca. Okay.

They went into Maurice's room but she waited outside.

Caro was surprised when they said that she had to go in the ambulance as well. If Bridget and Luis got back and there was no one there, what would happen? The ambulance men had Maurice connected up and plugged into a machine. Caro felt sick with the movement of the vehicle. Had buses and trains been like this? She didn't think so but it was hard to recall.

In the hospital she was put in a room and they asked questions. Who was Maurice's next of kin? Next of kin? She wasn't sure. Maurice had Bill, she said, but he died and he wasn't next of kin anyway. How long had she lived with him for? Was it just them? Who was his GP? GP? She didn't know. She had never known Maurice to go to the doctor's in all the time they'd been in the house. I looked after him, Caro had said. And who is your GP? She gazed at the sign on the door. Who is your GP? I don't know, she said. There's nothing wrong with me.

They kept her in for two days. She knew she should have tried to get back to the house because there was nothing to prevent her from leaving. But she was in a room with other people and when she ran her hand along the sheets, felt the bulk of the pillow, the bed was beautiful. They brought her tea on a tray and beside the bed there was a jug of water. They had even put ice-cubes in it and given her two straws in the glass.

It was the police who took her back to the house to pick up her stuff. In the car the policewoman gave Caro a polo mint. Nothing to worry about, she said, but the police went into the house first. Anyone home? they shouted. There was silence. Looks like your friends have been and gone, the woman said.

They wanted to see Maurice's room.

Why? Caro asked the woman.

We'd just like to see it.

Up here, then.

What are those buckets? the policewoman asked.

She looked more closely.

Oh, she said.

She pulled the curtains wide, throwing light on a threadbare carpet, a spindly wooden chair and a little chest of drawers. A spring protruded from the stained and thin mattress.

This one their room? the policeman shouted from the hall.

When Caro peeped in, she saw the TV at the bottom of Bridget and Luis's bed and a huge stack of DVDs. Piled high on the bed were frilled white cushions that could have been in a country cottage.

So where was it that you slept, Caroline? she said.

They went down the hall.

Okay, the policeman said. What were you doing with that thing? He pointed at the tent in the middle of the room.

The tent was comfortable. And more importantly it was warm. She had got used to sleeping in it and she liked it. Luis had brought it back one day.

Can see it would be freezing, he said. You've never thought of getting that broken window fixed instead?

Caro looked at the window. The frame had rotted away

at one side and part of the window had fallen out. How long ago? She couldn't remember. She hardly noticed it anymore.

No.

Okay, well let's go back downstairs again, shall we? the woman said.

At that point another man arrived but he was just in ordinary clothes. Everyone had moved to the kitchen. The new man said, Good washing machine you have there. He looked at the poster that was on the wall in the kitchen. Who's he? he said.

Samora Machel, Caro said.

He live here too?

No, Caro replied. Samora Machel. He led the Liberation Front against Portugal.

Oh? said the man, looking again at the picture. Samora Machel. That's right. Of course.

They let Caro gather her few things from her room. But what about my friends? she said. They're going to wonder where I am. They're going to wonder where Maurice is.

We'll let them know, the man replied. When we find them.

Caro imagines that in Belfast there are buildings like the one they took her to, a monument of grey and glass. There will be buildings like that in the city centre, but she hasn't been there yet. Only a twelve-minute journey: she has looked it up on her phone. She sees the 6A bus frequently. It moves at a friendly, unhurried pace. She'll move beyond the road reasonably soon. There's Donegall Square, she has seen it in Maps on her phone, and she intends to go to a café there, read a book or a magazine, then get the bus back. But although there was so much glass on the outside, the room she was taken to had no windows at all.

What was going on? Could she explain it? She wasn't to be frightened. There was nothing to fear. Just explain it so that everyone could understand what had been going on. The woman twisted the cross around her finger. Just explain it all right from the beginning. Relics of words of ideas of the past; socialist collective, dismantling of, dismantling of whatever it was, non-traditional living, whatever it was.

Well, whatever it was you were doing, you were doing at the expense of somebody else. The man was angry and the vein on his right temple almost pulsed. Mr Harrison locked away upstairs in his cell, pissing into a bucket, fed slop while everybody else is spending his money, living in his house, lazy bastards, no fucking medication in all those years? Mr Harrison's house, left to him by his old mother, money coming out of his bank account month after month, poor bastard had practically nothing left and he was well-off at one time, all those cheques, all those withdrawals, plus what they were claiming as well, incapacity, disability, housing benefit, parasitic fuckers. You had no idea? Socialist collective you said, didn't you? Don't make me laugh. He got up to leave the room but then sat down again. Do you know where they were? The other two? At a boutique hotel in Brighton. One night special with champagne on arrival. A boutique hotel in Brighton where every room is done out like a different Bond film, comrades Luis and Bridget, bottle of fizz in the Octopussy room, although stuck in a room with a bottle of fizz and that fat cunt, think I'd use it to knock myself out. That man was nearly dead, and you were living in a fucking tent, you total and utter and complete fucking idiot. Don't speak like that, the woman with the cross said. You can't speak to her like that. Oh yes I can, he said. I'll speak to her however I want just at present.

The hostel was next, the hostel that had the kitchen where two teenage girls just out of care were always making toast. The girls talked to each other but not to anyone else. A woman who was crying all the time because she didn't have her children sobbed into wet kitchen roll. Caro set out the breakfast things round the big communal table even though nobody ever sat at it. One day a balding man in a beige coat turned up. Caroline, he said. She looked blank. It's me. He said he would be back again in a few weeks once he had got everything ready and she wasn't to panic, because he'd be back. She wasn't likely to panic because the hostel suited her well enough, sitting in the room for hours on end with no one requiring anything at all from her.

Belfast, the voice said, temperature in Belfast, weather in Belfast, taxi from the airport to Belfast, but it might have been Mars, the clouds out the window white as new trainers. He showed her photos of his wife and daughter on a beach and sitting round a table in a restaurant. The daughter looked like him. No longer with us, you know, he said, Mum and Dad, no longer with us. Sorry, she said. Yeah, well, that's the way it goes. I don't live far from the old house. You won't be living far from the old house. It seemed centuries since she'd seen them and she couldn't conjure up their faces even fleetingly.

Caro gets out one of her books. She sharpens her pencil and turns to a new page of her jotter. She'll focus today. Pressing her fists against her temples, she recalls the first chapter of this book and how it's important. The second chapter moves to offer contextualisation—interesting but not essential. This first one though requires concentration. She wonders if a cup of tea would help. She is still stuck on the Taste of Manila on her game app. In the margin of her book she writes out again the six letters that are refusing to form themselves into a word. She writes them out again, the vowels first, then the consonants. There's someone at the door. It can't be the pizza because she hasn't ordered it yet. There's a local election coming up and the parties are leafleting. It's maybe just a rattle at the letterbox and then a quick departure.

Aunt Caroline!

The niece has got a rucksack with her, and bobbing on the bottom of it is a rolled up sleeping bag.

Hi! she says. She has had her hair cut, a section shaved at the side.

Oh, Caroline says. It's you.

The niece drops the rucksack on the floor and collapses into the sofa.

Okay, well, I've fallen out with Dad, she says. Like, I've really fallen out with him. I was wondering if I could sleep here. I won't be any trouble. Honest. I got my own sleeping bag and everything. It's from Duke of Ed. You know all that stuff, going to the Mournes, cooking over a fire.

I've even brought stuff for us to eat. Look. She pulls out a packet of biscuits and a bag of popcorn from the top of the rucksack.

Thanks, Caro says. Popcorn.

I'll be no bother at all. I can just put the sleeping bag down in here, yeah?

Sure, says Caro. If you think it's a good idea.

She makes them both a cup of tea and the niece opens the biscuits.

I was telling people at school about you, she says. Some of them didn't believe me. They were like, no way. So I looked you up.

There was a bit on you. Not loads like. A bit. The wee man didn't die did he?

No, Caro says. He didn't die.

Where is he now?

Being cared for somewhere. I don't know where.

I saw the pictures of Fat Cat. Was she gay? Pretty much everybody I know is gay, or bi. You heard of pansexual?

Caro isn't sure she has.

Well, anyway, the niece continues. I saw a programme about Patti Smith. Know who she reminds me of? You. Although she wasn't in a house like you were, being controlled and all that. But, you know. Same difference. You went away off and did your own thing. And so did she. So it's alright if I stay here? she says.

Caro pauses. Is there no one else you would rather stay with?

There's a rash of spots that run along the girl's hairline

and Caro could reach out to touch them with something close to a tenderness. But instead she unrolls the sleeping bag. You sleep in my room, Caro says, I'll sleep on the floor. It's absolutely fine.

Caro thinks that when she gets the chance she will phone her brother to let him know his daughter is here and that she is going to have a pizza and then she is going to stay the night. But she would like him to pick her up early in the morning before she goes to the Polish shop.

Nostalgie

The night before, Drew has a smoke on the promenade deck of the Liverpool–Belfast boat. The sky, barred pink and yellow, is almost psychedelic and he thinks about getting his phone out to photograph it for Jan, before deciding not to bother. He hadn't asked her to come, even though she'd pointed out that she hadn't ever seen much of Ireland. This particular trip, he said, didn't warrant the effort. When she asked what type of concert it was, he replied, although it wasn't entirely true, that all he knew was when and where he needed to turn up.

Drew drops his final cigarette into the night sea and heads back to the cabin, a family type, with two sets of bunks. He looks at its wood laminate as he drinks the bottle of whiskey he bought, thinking of all the holidays the four of them have taken over the years: the beds in hotels, villas and cottages that had been theirs for a week or so. A surprise that their almost-adult kids came on that last one to Cyprus. The promise of winter sun. One night, in the hotel bar, a waiter passed plastic sheets round the tables, lists of songs for karaoke. When he brought the next tray of drinks, Drew handed the lists back to him.

The cabin is a luxury. He could easily have slept for a few hours on one of the lounge chairs. But he wants to enjoy the journey, as he trips back. He knows it's pathetic in a way, but he doesn't care. That night, at the karaoke, the singers were drunk and pitiful, apart from one woman, not terribly young, who sang so beautifully the room went preternaturally quiet. When she finished, Drew realised he'd been holding his breath. His eyes were wet. He saw the woman afterwards, loading deckchairs and other beach paraphernalia into the boot of her car.

Drew keeps drinking, the dark pressing on the single porthole. His thoughts slide, as they habitually do when he's alone with them, to Delphine, even though it's decades since he's seen her. The time spent recollecting being with her adds up to more than the actual duration. 'With her' is a misnomer. He leapt on flights, chased her all over the place. Insane really, but he'd liked the intensity. Jan saw a picture of her in the paper years later. She's not as pretty as I thought she'd be, she said. But Delphine was never pretty. She was magnificent. Thinking about her all these years later is still exciting.

Drew doesn't know what the technical-set up will be at the hotel, but then he's only singing four or five songs. The tracks with his vocals scrubbed were easy to get sorted. He found his album in a box in the roof-space, wedged between the old cot and the Christmas decorations. He swapped the cover with the name Drew Lord Haig for the anonymity of a black liner sleeve. But he needn't have feared mockery: the young guy at the studio had barely looked at him.

Ludicrous to wonder, there in the cabin, where it all went wrong because, by multiple indexes, what he has now is success. In the early nineties, he'd retrained in IT and started earning good money. Only rarely does he come across anyone who remembers his previous incarnation. He'd gone on to set up his own company. Meticulous and reliable, their retention of trade is almost one hundred per cent. He's got a nice house that has tripled in value over the last fifteen years, great kids and a wife he loves. Drew watches with contempt those contemporaries of his who persevere with projects that are no more than end-of-the-pier shows.

But where *did* it all go wrong? He settles back on the bunk. With zero interest in writing some lumpen song about standing in a benefits queue, Drew sang instead about sex and death, disillusionment and ennui. His tenor voice, despite having no training, was operatic; he embraced excess in both sentiment and arrangement. 'Tale of the Shady Lane' was in the Top 30 in 1984. Its B-side, a nihilistic affair called 'Nostalgie de la Boue', borrowed that phrase for an attraction to what is depraved or degrading. It sounded good. Drew appeared on television. Although never dreamboat handsome, he was an attractive enough figure in a black turtleneck. His hooded eyes looked world weary and in the few interviews he did, he intimated a complicated past which he had not had.

His manager was Nicky Larner, a woman with a machine-gun voice. Ever since, he has been wary of people who speak quickly as a means of convincing the universe they are dynamic individuals. But back then he was flattered by Nicky and her promises of what was just around the corner. She encouraged him to go on a pointless, sprawling US tour as a support act. When he returned, there were new faces on the scene, brighter, hotter, shinier. Drew had the creeping realisation he was out of fashion, already. His album, recorded quickly and carelessly, got no exposure and didn't do well. He continued with dwindling conviction for another few long years before deciding to retreat from that world entirely.

And so, when a few months ago, he got an email that began 'Dear Drew Lord Haig' he was surprised. Lord, his mother's maiden name, he had originally inserted to suggest something of the déclassé degenerate aristocrat. For so long now, he has been, simply, Drew Haig. The email came from someone in Northern Ireland of all places, a man called Jimmy Henderson; it asked if he was available for singing at parties. Drew ignored it. Another email arrived the week after, this time with a particular date. Drew gave a polite but insistent no, thanking Jimmy Henderson for his interest. Within a few days came another. The ex-brigadier, Jimmy wrote, was particularly keen that Drew should perform at the centenary of the battalion. Their only stipulation: that he should perform one song, which was the battalion anthem, as it were. It was spelt Nastalji Della Boo.

The totally risible money that Jimmy offered was irrelevant. Drew was amazed that, in the depths of nowhere, there were people who knew, what, an album track, a B-side from over thirty years ago! Almost beyond belief. Drew didn't have much interest in Ireland but he gave the battalion's Wikipedia page a quick scan. Now disbanded, they had in the past been responsible for a number of deaths.

Still, they hadn't been active for a couple of decades at least. There was a photograph of the organisation's one-time leader, shaking hands in the nineties with a member of the government. By chance, Drew watched a current affairs programme where someone, a very attractive woman actually, wondered if those far removed from a situation, in their position of peaceful privilege, should sit in judgement on individuals who took particular actions in a specific place during a certain period in history. And so he wrote back to say yes, he would come.

Drew sleeps well in the little cabin. In the morning, when he rolls off the ferry, he parks the car at the dock area in Belfast and walks around for a while, taking in the sights of the new quarter, its hotels and building sites, its urban housing. Across the spangled lough he can see the film studio that once was the shipyard paint hall. He has a coffee down at a waterside café and watches a couple, young and in love, seemingly, from the time that they walk towards him to when they become figments in the distance. Eventually, he goes back to the car and starts his journey to the hotel. Heading down the motorway, he practises singing along to the songs, surprised at how easily the words come back to him. His voice, he feels, sounds good. It has a slightly sad timbre that he could only have tried to emulate in his twenties.

When Drew gets to the hotel, he phones Jan but she's dashing out to meet a friend and so can't speak for long. The place isn't particularly picturesque—just an old building, with cumulative additions over the years, in various bricks and styles. It's surrounded by farmland. Drew goes to his room and hangs the clothes he is intending to wear over a chair: a shirt the kids had bought him for his birthday one year, and a pair of black trousers he sometimes wears to meet work clients.

He feels like going down to the bar. The main entrance to it is at the back of the hotel. It has a hard, spartan aesthetic of the type that people would spend a lot of money trying to replicate. Drew orders a pint and sits at a table in front of a television, which shows horse-racing. There are few people around, other than a middle-aged couple having some food. Drew thinks that he should maybe eat too, and so orders a sandwich. The old barman polishes glasses and changes a keg. Drew watches him do these things.

It seems a pleasant and plain old bar and he enjoys the time he spends there that afternoon, the watery sunlight coming through high windows, the only sound the racing commentary. It seems remote, that research on a computer screen. As Drew watches the barman polish glasses and change a keg, or exchange friendly words with the couple as they get up to leave, it is as distant as newspaper reports of internecine strife in Syria or the Congo.

When the evening finally comes, Drew takes his time getting ready. He shaves carefully, guides his hair into a little quiff, polishes his shoes, slowly buttons his shirt. The arrangement is that he will meet Jimmy Henderson in the hotel foyer. So Drew stands in front of a rack of brochures about the local area until someone shouts his name. Jimmy Henderson, warm and friendly, takes him through to the function room where the centenary celebration will take place. Drew gives him the drive with the sound files and Jimmy Henderson stares at it. The music, Drew says. Jimmy nods and tells him that he will get one of the young lads to sort it out.

It's a fine name you got, Jimmy declares. Drew Earl Haig.

Lord Haig, says Drew.

We lay numerous poppy wreathes every year, Jimmy replies. Numerous.

The function room suggests a downbeat high-school prom. Suspended in one of the corners is a lone helium balloon. Tables are arranged around a little platform made up of wooden boxes covered with black canvas. The one microphone has tinsel wrapped around it. Behind the bar in this room is the same man Drew had watched earlier. They nod over to each other like old friends.

Before long, people begin to drift in and take their seats. They are mainly men. Many of them are ancient and shrunken, their jackets meant for wider shoulders. One is in a wheelchair, a tartan rug across his lap, and another, connected to a plastic tube, trails behind him a frame with some kind of oxygen canister. But there are younger people, some in pristine sportswear, their arms taut with muscle, and a few women too. Jimmy Henderson sees Drew looking at the redhead in tight leather.

That's Angie Pin-Up, Jimmy says. Angie, come here a minute, would you?

When she's standing next to Drew, he sees that she is the same age as him, if not older.

It's great you were able to come over, Angie Pin-Up says. We're all looking forward to hearing the song. You know, actually sung, by you.

Drew thanks her and says how much he is going to enjoy singing tonight. Jimmy Henderson gives Angie Pin-Up the drive with the music and asks her to get it sorted with one of the guys. Drew asks if there is going to be a sound check.

Ah no, says Jimmy Henderson. We don't need to stand on ceremony.

People continue to appear, greeting each other with bear-hugs or handshakes, depending on age. Several, when they arrive, go over to the frail individual with the oxygen. They clasp his hand. One man, solid as steak, even kisses him on the head. The drink is cheap and strong and, like the night before, Drew has moved onto whiskey. His performance, he knows, will not benefit from him being sober. Drew had assumed there would be other acts, but he is, it seems, the sole attraction.

At a certain point, when the room is full, Jimmy Henderson comes over to the table where Drew sits, to say that the brigadier has given the word that he should begin. Jimmy indicates a man, sitting with Angie Pin-Up. Drew, on the box stage, introduces himself to a little polite applause. What then follows, however, is a malfunction that causes the sound to cut out. People start talking again. Drew stands there, awkward, microphone in hand. But, when the music is restored, he begins once more.

He starts with his nearest thing to a hit, 'Shady Lane', and as the backing track plays, he thinks, as he has done so many times before, what a mistake it was to have that organ at the beginning. It's too insistent. But still the people carry on talking, so even from the stage Drew can hear the clink of glasses at the bar, the laughter at the tables. Men continue arriving, weaving their way through the tables, greeting this and that person. Drew does another two songs from his album. They seem so mannered and ridiculously baroque. He swallows the vocals, embarrassed and impatient to be done, looking with envy at that balloon, aloof, where the wall meets the ceiling.

But then everything changes. With the first few bars of 'Nostalgie', his final song, absolute silence descends. And, as he continues, people begin to sing along. They know every word. When it comes to the chorus, a great, magnificent crescendo rings out as they hold their drinks high to sing, 'Nostalgie, Nostalgie, Nostalgie de la boue'. On the final refrain the sound swells louder again. 'Nostalgie de la boue!' As Drew finishes, they leap to their feet, those that can, to applaud. Some of the younger ones start chanting what he takes to be the initials of their organisation.

Once the applause is finally over, Drew leaves the function room and goes outside. His fingers tremble as he lights his cigarette. That one song! It was remarkable! He could hardly remember, even in his early days, a response like that. Life glorious and at full tilt: it's not so very dead and gone.

Someone is beside him. It's the old barman and he has brought Drew another drink. He sets it down on the one outdoor table.

On the house, he says.

Thanks very much, Drew replies.

You did well in there.

Really was incredible, how it ended up going down!

They've always loved that song.

Well, says Drew, they must be the only people in the world.

Been their song since the eighties. Their anthem. Their theme tune.

That long? Incredible.

Yeah.

Amazed they'd ever heard of it.

Jim tell you the story?

No.

Bar you were in this afternoon, used to be a jukebox there. Beautiful old thing, American, all lit up. They walked in, the four of them, after they'd done The Hill Haven. And somebody, Christ knows who, put that tune on. Hit the wrong button. Didn't matter, it became their song from that night.

Terrible, he said. The Hill Haven. But, a month earlier it had been the McGowans killed on their farm.

He lifted two empty beer bottles and took them inside.

Drew takes his phone from his pocket, looks up Hill Haven. He reads about the men with assault rifles. The two eighty-year-olds dead. And the mother of three. And the boy of thirteen earning pocket money, collecting glasses. There is a picture of blood-streaked linoleum, shards from a shot mirror. The footsteps he can hear are Jimmy Henderson's.

We wondered where you'd got to, Jimmy says. They're

begging you to come in and sing our song one more time, Drew.

Oh no, he says, putting his phone back in his pocket.

But you must.

No. I sang it for you and that's it.

But you have to. You have to.

The response is even more impassioned the second time. 'Nostalgie de la boue!' rings out into the night. The frail old man with the oxygen particularly wants to thank Drew— he stretches out his hands to embrace him—but Drew's arms remain folded. He gives Jimmy a quick nod when the brown envelope of cash is handed to him. Back at the hotel, Drew sees he has missed calls from Jan, but he doesn't ring her back.

As soon as it is light, he drops the hotel key in the empty reception and sets off for the city. He has no cabin on the return journey and so he moves between the cafe and the lounge area. He even watches a film that is showing, a comedy that involves a dog show. Halfway across the Irish Sea, there is still a phone signal that allows Jan to call again. Yes, he says, he'll be home after seven. Burgers or carbonara? Whatever, he says. Alright, maybe the carbonara.

He doesn't want another coffee in the cafe. He doesn't want to see another film. Drew takes a look around the shop with its bottles of perfume and shelves of whiskies, goes out on the promenade deck for a smoke. When the rain gets too heavy, he goes back inside. On his way to the lounge he sees the gaming area, a congress of machines, their lights lurid and flashing in the dim. Drew stands in front of one with a backlit and saturated image of a scantily clad woman leaning against a limousine. He takes out the brown envelope from his pocket and feeds one of the notes into the machine which triggers a crescendo of gurgling sound. He spins the reel. Loses. The eighty-year-olds having a quiet drink. Spins the reel. Loses. The mother of three, those kids of hers. Spins the reel. Loses. The child collecting glasses, saving for something from the catalogue. The rest of those notes, he feeds them in, hoping to lose over and over again.

Memento Mori

The books in the library are fairly limited: mainly true crime and thrillers. Every so often Gillian fills in a transfer request for titles of interest and, within three or four weeks, they come. Most frequently she asks for books about gardens because although there's a small plot here, opportunities are limited. In terms of other reading material, it usually takes a couple of days before she gets the Sunday paper but she's used to that now. And, anyway, she focuses so little on the actual news that it wouldn't matter, a paper one week, two weeks old.

On the last page of the magazine supplement a woman, in response to a problem or supposed difficulty, gives circumlocutory and banal advice that spans a number of paragraphs. Tracey used to read it out loud every Sunday. She'd be lying on the sofa and the fire would be lit. Her own counsel was blunt. My advice to this person is basically to wise the fuck up, she'd say. Gillian pretended to wince, but really, in most circumstances it would have been beneficial for the people to take heed. Yet there were times when someone who seemed a prime candidate for harsh pragmatism was treated with a degree of kindness, because he or she reminded Tracey of somebody she used to know, in London, in Liverpool, in other lives. And so, when Gillian eventually does get the Sunday paper on a Tuesday or Wednesday, she reads the problem page first and thinks of Tracey.

Tracey used to say, Gillian, what in the name of god did you do before you met me? It surprised her that Gillian had been with so few people. Gillian always replied that she had simply been waiting for her. Thinking now, that does seem the way of it. Sitting in a café in a foreign city, watching a young couple in the park, in the dark of the cinema, when she had to put down a book because its evocation of some or other passion was so acute, she had all along been dreaming of Tracey, although she had yet to meet her. Tracey, by contrast, had had plenty of previous partners, had even been married once. It was never going to work out, she said. Too young, too crazy. Lucky we got a year and a half out of it!

Of all places, a book launch was where they met. Gillian's old friend Wendy had written some short stories. The launch took place at a bar down near the docks, which had not yet succumbed to anyone's notion of a new Belfast. Wendy and her husband had filled said bar with vases of lilies but still the smell of stew lingered. Gillian was at a table with a ragbag of people, some who worked with her friend, a few neighbours, a taxi driver Wendy regularly used. Although they had all bought the book, dutifully, they agreed that they didn't read short stories, or even like them all that much. Then another person joined them. She said that when Wendy next came in for a blow dry, she would just get her to tell the stories and that would save the bother of reading them. Tracey was Wendy's hairdresser.

There was dancing upstairs at the launch. Prancing about in a pokey room above a pub was the last thing Gillian would enjoy, but that was where Tracey had been. The blonde hair framing her face was damp. She said she had to go because she was working early in the morning and did anyone fancy sharing a taxi? No one did. Gillian said that she was leaving anyway and that, if she wanted, she could give Tracey a lift to wherever she needed to go.

Because she doesn't like fussiness, people assumed wrongly that Gillian was uninterested in fashion. The simplicity of her present attire is in fact pleasing to her, representing as it does merely a higher degree of the functional and clean lines, often Belgian, that she would have chosen herself anyway. On one occasion, during the first few weeks of their being together, Tracey said she would give Gillian a transformation. She reluctantly agreed. Tracey refused to let Gillian look in the mirror as she poured her into a tight dress in blue crushed velvet. Tracey painted her face with a range of implements, keeping up a running commentary that meant nothing to Gillian, about the products and the size of the brushes, the techniques she was using. She placed Gillian's feet into stilettos. And then the full-length mirror was spun around. Ta dah! Tracey said. Gillian looked a different creature. Her eyes, ringed with black, took in her legs, her waist, the size of her mouth. You're beautiful, huh? Tracey said. I did always know, she said. From the first time I saw you. But you are better the way you are. And so Gillian took off the dress, and then the shoes.

That night of the launch, Tracey realised, when they had driven to her flat, that she'd forgotten her keys. She emptied everything from her bag onto the rubber mat: hairsprays, make-up, a jotter, a handful of bills, a birthday card, but no keys. She said, not to worry, one of her neighbours had a spare set, but when she rang his bell, he wasn't there. Tracey kept saying how she could just visualise the keys sitting on the table in the kitchen. But she didn't want to hold Gillian up; she could walk around for a while until the neighbour got back. He'd probably just nipped to the garage shop. Gillian said she was in no rush and Tracey asked if there was anyone waiting for her at home. No, just me, Gillian said. She'd looked after her mother, but she was gone now. Eventually, when the neighbour had still not returned an hour later, Gillian said it wouldn't be a problem if Tracey wanted to stay the night at her house. It was only a short drive away.

What happened next, remembered so many times, is burnished and glittering and perfumed. The dark's velvety and there's the scent of honeysuckle from the garden, fresh and lovely, although it's not the time for it. Nightingales sing, the moonlight catches on Tracey's cheeks, and the house welcomes her, with a sigh of relief because she is finally home. When Gillian brought the tea, she was on the sofa, shoes off and her legs curled under her. Matching mugs and coasters! she said. You neat freak! She was right. All the same shade of slate. Tracey's laugh rang out. Later, Gillian dragged a quilt down the stairs but Tracey asked if she didn't have a double bed. Well then, save yourself the hassle of sorting anything cos l can just sleep beside you. Gillian must have looked alarmed because Tracey said, Don't worry, I'm not gonna pounce in the middle of the night. Relax! But Gillian lay there, long after Tracey had fallen asleep, hoping that she would wake and pounce in whatever way she felt like.

Gillian goes to classes, three a week. One she would broadly term ethics, another mindfulness and the third is upholstery. She prefers the upholstery class because it makes the most sense. The mindfulness teacher is forever asking them to consider the moment but Gillian sees her eyes slide to the clock on the wall with some regularity. Gillian would prefer the physicality of the moment with the stapling gun. The ethics course, taken by an ex-minister, tends to be reductive. It begins with an exegesis of a biblical text, so the framework for any inquiry relating to right and wrong is established in a particular way from the beginning. Today is unusual, however, because she has a couple of visitors.

Tracey didn't really leave, after that night. She preserved the illusion of still having her own flat for a month or so, and Gillian made some quasi-metaphorical observations about her needing her own space. But she didn't. And Gillian didn't. It was simple. They were together. A lot changed. In work Gillian had greater reserves of patience for tasks and people she usually found wearisome. She even took delight in them now and then. With Tracey, Gillian went on holidays to places she would never normally have visited.

Tracey liked bargains, deals, vouchers, menus that ended at unlikely times like 7.20 pm, brightly coloured drinks. They watched preposterous films, ate everything fried, covered things in sriracha. Tracey would send lewd text messages about what she wanted to do to her right now this red-hot minute. Gillian rarely responded in kind although she loved to get them. Gillian would suggest walks in some wild, blasted spot. Is there a coffee shop nearby? Tracey would enquire. Or, better still, a bar?

And then. And then they were in Majorca, Tracey's choice, and Gillian wanted to go to some chapel she had read about. Tracey's idea was to find a Sephora shop. In the cool hush of the church Gillian saw she'd got a message from her and she hoped it was something lewd and explicit and that she was waiting in the hotel for her right now. Instead, it was Tracey saying that she didn't feel great. That's why she had headed back to the room. Tracey was tired for the rest of that holiday. They ended up both pushing the food around their plates in the same restaurant every night. When they returned home, Tracey went back to work but she had no energy. She was losing weight. The doctor said that maybe it was an iron deficiency. They got a stash of supplements.

Tracey had started getting bruises, the size of fingerprints. But she could never remember where or when or how she might have hit herself. Gillian got arnica for them, put the cream gently on Tracey's arms and knees, the insides of her legs where the skin was so soft. Eventually the hospital referral came. She went, got the tests, and they waited. Gillian has grown arnica. It can handle less than ideal conditions. She's grown it here.

The diagnosis, when it came, was worse than they expected. Gillian said all the things that people come out with in such circumstances. Was there any chance it could be wrong? Were there places in the States that offered treatment? The doctor tipped his head a little, gave a sad smile and said he didn't think so. But stage four? How could that have happened? It was incredible! Surely it didn't work like that? What about chemo? Did everybody not get chemo? This was ridiculous.

Oh well! Tracey said. It was good while it lasted.

Here for a good time, not a long time, she added, when the doctor and Gillian offered no response.

They returned in silence to the hospital car park. I can't believe you, Gillian said. I can't remember a time I heard something more inappropriate. Joking like that. Totally not the time or the place.

Tracey made a face.

I mean, how, Tracey, has this even happened? How could you not have had an inkling that you were so sick? You must have done. The whole thing is nothing short of unbelievable.

Well, know what I can't believe? Tracey said. I can't believe you. I've just found out I'm ill, big-time ill, like, on-the-way-out-style ill, and you're giving me a hard time over it? That's what the fucking joke is. She shook her head. Don't even speak to me. I mean it, Gillian, I don't even want you to say a word to me, she said. It was the only time they ever fell out, that day at the hospital.

In the early hours, Gillian slipped out of bed and went down to the kitchen which was peaceful, unsympathetic even, in its quiet order. She didn't believe in divinities or gods. She knew that in the grand scheme all's meaningless, that everything is flux, patternless. Still, she was furious at a cosmic order she knew didn't exist. To only allow them two years! To grant them only that? The epic gave way to the banal. The bulbs planted in the garden that Tracey wouldn't see pushing through. That film they were looking forward to seeing that wouldn't be out until next year. Why not go outside and howl, lie down in the dirt and scream at a black sky, kick and kick and kick and punch punch punch.

At what? Air?

In the morning, Gillian cooked breakfast and made a list of what needed to be done. In work, she spoke to her bosses to discuss what could be put in place over the next months to allow her to be at home to care for Tracey. They were good. They had ideas. When she got back at the end of the day, she mowed the grass and cut the hedge with the electric clippers. In the evening she read everything she could about what was happening to Tracey.

One Wednesday morning Gillian was working from home. She had checked on Tracey a couple of times but she was asleep. There was time to get to the shops, only a short walk away, to pick up a prescription. While she was there, she would get a few of those splashy gossip magazines that Tracey liked so much. On the walk home, as she turned the bend of their road and the house came into view, Gillian saw a crowd of people. A police car crawled past, its siren a slow wail. When Gillian got nearer, she saw that the police had cordoned off an area with tape and that, outside their house, there was a white tent. It resembled the kind of pagoda seen on upmarket beaches.

What's happening? Gillian asked a woman who was standing against the tape, watching the tent.

Somebody's been beheaded, she said. Someone's been beheaded by Boko Haram.

Gillian doubted that. This didn't really seem the spot for it. Boko Haram diversifying operations from West Africa to Ardenlee Gardens seemed unlikely. Still, there was a tent and a team in forensics suits. The tape was right across their driveway.

She asked someone else, a neighbour, have you any idea what's happening?

He said that someone had been stabbed. A young girl. Dead. She was there, in the tent. They hadn't brought her out yet.

Gillian stood there for about twenty minutes, along with everyone else. It was a terrible thing that had apparently happened to a young girl, but she was also thinking about Tracey and how she would wake up and find her not there. She went over to one of the policemen and asked how long it would be before she could get into her house. She pointed in its direction.

How long is a piece of string? he said. This is a serious incident.

I realise that, Gillian replied. I mean, it's appalling, whatever's happened. But I really do need to get into my house.

He said he would find out from someone what the situation was regarding access to her house and so she waited for him to return. People in white suits were going in and out of the tent. She rang Tracey but there was no answer. Gillian moved to duck under the tape but the policeman she had spoken to appeared from nowhere to say that she wasn't permitted to do that. He put his hand on her arm, as if to restrain her.

Do you mind? she said. I need to get in here because somebody is seriously ill.

A policewoman was called over and she said that she would accompany Gillian. Perhaps this someone inside the house might have seen something.

I doubt it, Gillian said. She's ill.

The policewoman asked Tracey a few questions anyway, although, as predicted, she knew nothing that could help. On the news that night, the report was of a fatal stabbing and their house appeared briefly on screen, a backdrop to the tent. Tied to the gate was a remnant of the police cordon, which fluttered a little in the wind. When Gillian went out the next morning, a number of cheap bouquets wrapped in cellophane had been left on the ground by their hedge. She'd never really liked cut flowers. They sucked the water greedily from the vase but they knew they were on the way out, dying as everyone admired their beauty. Cards were attached to a few of the ones here, the petals brown-edged already. One had RIP in fat, bubble handwriting and a name that Gillian couldn't read.

Later, Gillian sat beside Tracey on the bed to read aloud from the paper about the murdered girl who now had a name, Angelina Curran. She's so pretty, Tracey murmured, and she was, as glamorous as a starlet in her kitchen, the washing machine behind her. Just to be out, walking along, and then have something like that happen to you, Tracey said. All that day, increasing numbers of flowers were left by people, and also some cuddly toys. A teddy and some kind of rabbit had been pushed into the hedge. They stared out from it as though it was their habitat. It had rained by the afternoon and the folds of the cellophane wrapped around the flowers filled up with water.

They arrested someone quickly, Angelina's ex-boyfriend, a young man of nineteen. Strange again to see their house on TV, their hedge behind a close-up of the rabbit's face. During the days and the evenings, clusters of mourners appeared, some stunned, some weeping, hugging each other. The primary school where the girl had worked as a classroom assistant got its pupils to write messages, which were placed in plastic pockets and left where the hedge met the pavement.

A couple of days later, Gillian saw two older women there, standing in the rain. It was Angelina Curran's mother and auntie, looking at the spot where she had died. Gillian asked them if they wanted to come in, and they did. Other than when she lifted her cup of tea, the mother's hands were balled in fists. Gillian didn't tell them about Tracey upstairs. Why should she? They were only sitting on their sofa because of what had happened outside. These women had nothing to do with them. The auntie said, they hoped the boyfriend rotted in hell. Their family had welcomed him when his own didn't want to know. They lent him money. They were good to him. But when Angelina ended it, this is what he did. He was a bastard and their beautiful baby died in the street, the blood running out of her, and that evil cunt's face was the last thing she saw. Her voice rose, feral. Gillian said at the end that they were welcome to come back any time they wanted, although she half-hoped they didn't.

Today's visit from Toni Grey will be the usual chore. You know, Gillian, in this line of work, I've seen things you wouldn't believe. I've seen the lot and so on and so on and so on. That's how she talks. The last time Toni showed her a newspaper story about a film that was being shot in Belfast. And then another about some statue they had erected in County Down that had split public opinion. She asked Gillian what she thought of it. Environmental art is nearly always going to be controversial, she said. And then came newspaper article number three, a story about a woman who had died after being in a coma for four years as a result of being punched in the street. So, Toni said, what do you think of that? Very unfortunate, Gillian said. But then so much is. Don't you think, Toni?

Tracey kept saying that Gillian was doing a great job. Don't be making a fuss and getting other people involved. Gillian had wondered if they needed to get more help in terms of care. Tracey's parents visited every week, bringing bags of food that no one was ever going to eat. They didn't think much of the shrine outside. Fair enough, terrible about the wee doll, shocking, but this is your property, Gillian, at the end of the day. I mean, look at all the crap in that garden! Why not have the shrine where she lived rather than where she died? Would that not make more sense?

Angelina's mother and auntie, around again to see what people had left, came in once more for a cup of tea. Gillian told them this time that her partner was ill upstairs. She even said something like, it's terminal. The aunt asked her what age she was. Forty-three, Gillian said. She's due to be forty-four in August. Angelina was going to be nineteen in June, the mother said.

They still went out. They had hospital appointments. And Tracey wanted to see various things, like her old school, even though the building she knew had been replaced with a gleaming three-storey oblong. When they went to Tracey's parents' house, Gillian and Tracey sat in her old bedroom, a tiny box that looked out onto a backyard and which now housed a vacuum cleaner and bags of clothes to be taken to the charity shop. This little place, she said. All the things I thought about doing when I was lying in here. They must still be floating about, like fucking goldfish in a tank. One day they went to the salon where she used to work. Everyone was especially effervescent. They put her in the chair that was normally reserved for her clients and gave her a glass of champagne, well, cava. She couldn't bear to have her hair washed, so they just fluffed it out a little. Do Gillian's while you're at it, for Christ's sake, Tracey said. She needs it more than me! By that stage Tracey had lost so much weight.

When they returned that day from the salon, there was a small crowd outside the house in front of the driveway. Gillian waited for them to move, but these teenage girls were oblivious. One held some kind of music player. Gillian tooted the horn, lightly, briefly, and a couple of them turned to scowl. When no one moved, Gillian edged the car forward, causing them to shriek and scatter, apart from one individual who banged on the side of the car with something metal. When they got out, the girls shouted some insults. Get to fuck, Tracey said, without the force necessary for them to hear.

Nowadays, Gillian comes into contact with more young people—Arlene A, McCartney—than she has ever done since being young herself. They sometimes ask her advice, because she seems like a clever person. You got that vibe, Arlene A said one time. Like you've read a shitload of books. And also your hair kind of says clever. Gillian doesn't feel she has any good advice to give.

Florence was the one to tell them about Lola Fuentes, when she came to the house. Florence had briefly employed Tracey in her weave shop. I was just no good at it, Tracey said. Made everyone look worse rather than better. Florence laughed and didn't disagree. I saw all the Lola fans outside, Florence said. Who? Lola Fuentes. Who's that?

Surely another person hasn't been killed on our doorstep, Gillian said.

But no, Lola Fuentes was alive and kicking in Los Angeles. Or maybe New York. Florence couldn't remember exactly where it was she lived.

I know what she looks like, Tracey said, but I don't think I've actually ever seen her in anything. Can't remember, is she the one who used to be a dancer in tons of videos? Young girl, long black hair with a centre parting. Big eyes? That her?

Well, Florence said. There had been tons of photos of that poor Angelina in the papers and all over the place. Her Instagram was full of pictures. The kind of girl who loved dressing up. In half the photos you could still see the price tags of the clothes! One of those girls, god love her, sending off for stuff, photographing herself in it, sending it back. In one of the photos, yeah, Florence said, she's wearing a T-shirt and it had Lola Fuentes's face on it, you know one of those insane big close-ups of someone's face that takes up the entire T-shirt, and their eyeball is like the size of your whole boob? Well this photo was shared all over the place—I mean, she's so pretty, Angelina—and didn't Lola Fuentes, her actual self, see it! Florence said that at first there was apparently a bit of confusion because Lola Fuentes thought that Angelina was killed actually wearing that T-shirt, that she was stabbed through that shirt. But no, she had been wearing something else. Lola Fuentes had been a victim of domestic violence. She mentioned it in a lot of interviews. Other than the films, it was one of her things. So she had been talking about Angelina Curran all over the place, posting about her.

Among the flowers, the plastic and the sodden pieces of paper, when Gillian looked the next day, there were a few photos of the woman with long black hair in a centre parting. An old T-shirt had been tied to the gate. It was faded but she could see the washed-out shape of a face. Gillian undid it, and then brought it into the house. She used it later to clean the kitchen floor.

They came round again, the mother and the aunt. Even though it was some time still in the future, they wanted Gillian to know when the court case might be. They seemed to think that she might be called as a witness. Why? Because it happened in front of their hedge when she was at the shops? But she said nothing as they sat on the sofa and had another cup of tea. The mother cried and the auntie talked about how she wanted to see the guy imprisoned for the maximum length of time. In fact, she would have been happy to see the death penalty for him. He would have a good solicitor, of course, someone trying to make a name for himself and going on about his poor childhood blah blah blah and how he never had a mother, but that made no difference. When her voice rose, Gillian was scared she'd wake Tracey.

Her name aches in her mouth. Gillian says it in this little space, says it aloud: Tracey, Tracey. But when only the quiet hangs there, she wishes that she hadn't.

When Wendy comes to visit, they sit with the table between them. She isn't any more important to Gillian than other friends but she feels sentimental about the fact that she was the cause of her meeting Tracey. Wendy tells her that she is looking well. And Gillian says the same thing back. Gillian asks her some questions about her kids and about how work is going. That necessitates launching into a whole tale about Wendy being stranded in Glasgow when an airline went bust. She was there to do a book reading. Well, of course. So much segues into a discussion of that. Yet Gillian's pleased she's come to see her; it's a bit of a journey and she still can't drive. Wendy leaves it until the end to say something about how she feels that at the time she could have supported her more, should have done more, but Gillian bats this away. Don't be ridiculous, she says. Because there is no need to get mawkish over the whole thing. When she is back in her own space, Gillian curses herself for not asking more questions, for instance, what did Tracey talk about when she did Wendy's hair?

Tracey's mother let her sit in that old bedroom of hers for hours on end. She gave her most of the photos that she had. I don't mind you having them, Gillian, she said. I always hoped she'd meet someone like you. She was everywhere still in their house, the perfume of her. Although Gillian didn't wear make-up, she would dab on what had belonged to Tracey, ridiculous as it might have looked on her scrubbed, carbolic face. When Tracey died, she was in the hospice. They'd had to move her in the final few days. Her mother and Gillian were there. When Tracey died, well, that was it really.

The funeral and its arrangements were a burst of purposefulness, and Gillian did the job with absolute diligence, the phoning, organising, greeting, listening. At one point during the week after, when the house was open for visitors, the mother and aunt appeared, without seeming to realise that someone else had died. They talked again about the court case. It took Florence, who was there and pouring coffee for a couple of people, to say, I'm sorry love, but we are here for Tracey. You know, Tracey? The auntie's eyes widened. They left soon after.

And then came a point when there were no more people who needed to be handed a plate of biscuits. All the cards in hushed colours that were going to come had come, and they'd been placed in a box. Gillian got up one morning and there'd been a storm in the night. There were leaves stuck to the windows and the back garden was trashed with blossoms. She took a couple of black bin bags and went out of the front door. She gathered from the garden some rubbish that had blown there and the pieces of a flower pot that had blown over and smashed.

An old CD that had ended up under a bush went in the bag too. Gillian opened the gate and went out to look at the hedge. She worked methodically along the length of it, putting it all into the black plastic, the photos of Angelina, home-printed, the flowers, the cuddly toys with their now split seams, the cards, the messages in poly-pockets. It felt good to do it. There were people gutting a house in the next street and she knew that they had a skip outside, so she went round and swung the bag hard onto the assembled rubble and plaster board. It sent up a small cloud of cement dust. Gillian resolved to do the same thing every morning with a new black bin bag. Glad to see you back, they all said, when Gillian returned to work. They said she could take more time off but she was adamant. All tasks were completed with her customary precision.

Gillian gets told that Toni Grey can't come today. Instead, she sees the mindfulness person, who brings a snow globe to illustrate her point about the maelstrom of emotions in the mind. The snow looks like coconut. It's only Gillian with her today. The others are involved in something else. She asks Gillian to imagine running water and she thinks of a cold tap turned on full. I mean a waterfall, the woman says. Something beautiful. A waterfall tumbling into a lagoon.

Just a cold tap, Gillian says. Overflowing the sink now.

Counselling would still be an option for you, she says.

I know what would help, Gillian replies. The arrival of my library transfer. I'll check on its status later.

The shrine began to dwindle. Some mornings when she went out, there was practically nothing beyond one forlorn bunch of carnations and, really, Gillian didn't need a bin-bag anymore. But whenever the trial started, that changed. There was suddenly a new photo of Angelina everywhere: in the papers, on the news. In a simple white dress, she looked young and hopeful. There were shots of the mother and auntie walking quickly into the courthouse. And then there was the ex-boyfriend, bearded, a padded jacket over his suit, a policeman on either side of him. Lola Fuentes posted a video asking everyone to remember Angelina. She held a little candle. This video resulted in the resurgence of new materials left outside Gillian's house. The flames of the tea-lights were snuffed out by the wind almost as soon as they were placed on the ground. There was even a candle jammed into a wine bottle, that looked like it had been lifted from a restaurant.

It wasn't long before another relation came around. Not the mother, not the aunt, but an uncle. He wanted to ask Gillian to stop removing all the tributes that people had left for his niece. Gillian said she understood that they wanted to remember Angelina but it had now gone on for a long time.

This is our home, Gillian said. It's not really the place for a public memorial.

But, love, he said, it's not really your home. At the end

of the day. We're talking about a hedge and a pavement. That's public property.

Our hedge.

Well, we would like it if you didn't remove anything more.

To feel angry was a thrill. I'm actually not terribly concerned, she said, at the end of the day, about what you like or don't like.

His eyes were unblinking. Don't think you have totally got what I am fucking saying love, he said. Basically, this is me coming round having a nice talk with you before somebody else turns up that's not so nice, love. Uh huh? You understand?

Oh please send round whoever you feel like, she said. Don't delay.

On the final day of the trial, before the ex-boyfriend was found guilty of manslaughter by reason of diminished responsibility, Gillian was out buying plants for the garden, little seedlings. She had thought carefully about what she wanted to get. They looked vulnerable, those plants, with their little support stakes. On arriving back at the house, there were a few groups of people gathered already. The memorial was re-forming itself. One woman had a little sign saying Never Forget with a picture of Angelina underneath. The words were in red. Never Forget. Gillian asked the woman if she could get past. She was standing in front of their gate.

Justice for Angelina! she shouted.

You're in front of our gate, Gillian said.

Angelina, say her name!

Let me get past, please.

Gillian put down the plants she was holding in each hand. She brought her fist back so that it was level with her cheek and then propelled it forward. When it made contact with the edge of the woman's left eye, the relief and calm was overwhelming, a searing white. The woman fell, slow and heavy, to hit the kerb. Her right arm was extended almost to reach the latest tributes leaning against the hedge.

It's getting darker now and it will be lights out soon in Gillian's cell. Tomorrow will be another day much the same as all of the previous ones. That's fine; she has her various classes and gardening. She has her books to read. Sometimes, Gillian tells her own particular situation to Tracey in the style of the problem page at the back of the Sunday supplement. But in this instance, Tracey has no pragmatic or pithy advice. Oh love, is all she can say. Oh love, what a mess. She takes Gillian in her arms and they whisper to each other all the things that they never thought to say.

Secrets Bonita Beach Krystal Cancun

For the last nine years Linda and Rae had been having a takeaway together on a Friday night. Linda arrived at Rae's around half seven, and after the first glass of wine they put through their order which was the same every time. Always using the one takeaway, they were familiar enough with the food to be able to discern different workers. They gave them names. Mr Hot sprinkled chilli flakes on everything but Neatso wrapped up the boxes very precisely. There was one they called Olivia, after a girl Rae knew at school who was the worst in the class at cookery. Could've burnt an ice cube, Rae said. Olivia from the takeaway was of the same ilk: her ginger sometimes an inch thick, the onions almost quartered. The best though was the Boss. Great balance of flavours with the Boss, Rae always said. Great balance of flavours. The Boss knew what she was doing.

Rae lived by herself, and so did Linda since Danny had gone to university. Introduced by a mutual friend years ago, there had only been two occasions where they encountered each other outside the confines of Rae's house: once, their initial meeting at the mutual friend's when the Friday night arrangement was first suggested; and then at their mutual friend's wedding. At the wedding Rae wore her usual trainers, except in black. Her one concession to the event was a gold brooch in the shape of an owl. Linda thought that people at the wedding probably presumed that they were partners. Somebody at their table even said, you two should come around to ours some time. Linda didn't say that really they just had a takeaway together once a week.

Rae worked as a paramedic. When you look down and see that you still have the brains of the man from the motorbike accident on the toe of your boot, well, that's when you know you are doing a serious job, she said. She came out with this kind of comment quite often, considerations of the fragility of skulls, or how muscle turns black and viscous when burnt. It meant that Linda didn't often dwell on the various crises at the printers where she worked. Or anything else really. She didn't see blood run down drains in the road. In the whole time they had been meeting, she had only ever uttered Ritchie's name a handful of times. She couldn't be sure that Rae would actually even remember it.

One evening when Linda was round at Rae's, Rae said that Linda should maybe make other plans for the next week because she wasn't going to be around.

What do you mean? Linda asked.

I'm not going to be here. I'm meeting somebody.

What do you mean?

What do you mean, what do I mean? I'm meeting somebody for a drink. Not against the law.

On a Friday night?

You'll find, Linda, that the town is full of people meeting up for a drink on a Friday night.

Linda reached for another spoonful of the chicken dish from the plastic carton on Rae's coffee table.

Well, yeah, said Rae. Going for a drink. Nothing major. Just going to see how it goes.

So it's that kind of a drink, Linda said.

A drink's a drink. It's just with somebody I've been talking to online.

That Rae talked to guys online seemed quite incredible.

You'll need to be careful, won't you? Linda said.

Why's that? Rae asked.

Do you never read the papers?

Don't think I need to worry, Linda. I contacted him online but I didn't meet him online. Knew him from years ago. We used to work together.

I thought you said that all the guys you work with are next to useless.

We're not going to be working on Friday night.

Well, Linda said, just as long as you know what you're doing.

I do.

That's good then.

Rae put her plate down. Mike's like you, she said. Divorced.

Plenty of us around.

Plenty of you around making money for all the lawyers.

The only man that Linda ever looked for on the internet was her ex-husband. She searched for him every few days. There was another Ritchie Hart who lived in Cumbria and who did hill-walking, half-marathons for charity.

She had grown used to seeing his fresh and beaming face as he crossed another finish line. Linda was mostly relieved when she didn't see the sharp features of the one she was looking for or didn't come across his name in any newspaper's court reports. But when he appeared in none of her trawls, she was also disappointed. A brown envelope with their respective solicitors' letters was still about somewhere in the house, his woman's had the line drawing of the Georgian windows at the top, her man's one involved a configuration of semi-circles and triangles. When they split up, a person at work asked gently, did he have an affair? That wasn't it. An affair would have made it easier because she could have felt personally and particularly wronged. No, he certainly wasn't ever violent towards me, she had also had to say. I'd just had enough really. Enough of what? Just enough.

He got called a ladies' man which would suggest the type of person to have affairs but that was wrong because it was all about men. That was all it ever was about. The night when she was watching him dance with his boss at the time's wife: it was in one of the hotels in town, a Christmas do. She was pregnant with Danny. The boss's wife was drunk. And Ritchie was dancing with her slow and close. Her head flopped from one side to the other, blonde curls falling across her face, until it found a resting place on his shoulder. She reached up to loop her arms round his neck and then, and then he started running his hand up and down her back gently. The eyes of the other wives slid to Linda as she took a sip of her drink. One asked if she wanted to go to the toilet with her.

No, it's okay, Linda said.

Well, another woman said as she tried to laugh, he's certainly a bit of a ladies' man, that husband of yours.

But the point of the whole performance was the boss who was sitting over in a corner, seething, knuckles white, thinking about how he would escalate Ritchie to the final stage of disciplinary action before the month was out, the boss who, when the song was over, took his wife hard by the arm to lead her to their table. She turned to look at Ritchie, her hand half-raised in a wave, but he was already at the bar, his back to her. The other women felt sorry Linda knew, and if she left the table, they would start talking about her, so she continued to sit, smiling at jokes she could only partially hear.

No one more elegant than Ritchie, the way he danced. And how clothes just hung on him, everything draped perfectly. Once a mod always a mod, he said. Well, mod revivalist. Mod revival revivalist. Everything had to have the right number of buttons. He did his own washing, his own ironing, wouldn't let Linda near the stuff. She'd come downstairs and hear the slosh of the washing machine and know it would be Ritchie doing his clothes. There had been a laundry room, where he grew up. He mentioned it once or twice, how he liked the sound of the big industrial tumblers, the smell. He used to sleep, he said, on top of the tumblers, turn them on even when there was nothing in them, let them rumble him to sleep.

Mike's fatter than he used to be, Rae said. Fatter looking in his pictures anyway.

Well, you'll be seeing him in real life soon, Linda replied. And then you'll know for definite what size he is.

*

When the Friday evening came, rather than order a take-away to her own house Linda thought that there was no reason why she too shouldn't go into town. She parked the car in one of the multi-storeys and took a walk past the shops that were just shutting up for the evening. She could have been anywhere in the world and there wasn't a single soul who expected her to be in a certain place. That was freedom for you, liberation. She went to the doughnut place that was still open. It felt like a break-up place. Everything in it was destined to make it seem like that: the number of tables for just two, the low-key lighting, the temporariness of all the paper cups and plates. Someone had left a newspaper on the chair opposite her and so she read it while she had coffee and a doughnut filled with lemon curd.

There was a story about a young man who had had his leg amputated after a punishment shooting and who had been using his artificial limb as a bong. He was now up for drug-dealing. Linda looked at his not entirely doleful face, his slight smirk at the ridiculousness of it all. She leafed through the rest of the paper until she hit the sports section, then closed it. Back in the car park she watched a couple trying to load shopping into the boot of their car. The bags were awkwardly shaped and the boot already seemed stuffed with she didn't know what, carpets or rugs. Linda knew they would get it all in sooner or later but didn't want to leave until she saw it happen. The two gave each other a high-five when the boot was finally closed. And then Linda put her key in the ignition.

One time, when she'd only been going out with Ritchie

a few months, they were heading home after a night in a bar. He had been quiet for the duration of the evening, drinking in that efficient and unshowy way, vodka in a half pint glass, an inch of tonic. Suddenly, as they made their way down a dark avenue there was a high-pitched metallic grind and Linda realised that while one of Ritchie's hands was in hers the other held a set of keys that he had scored right along the length of the car they'd just passed.

What in the name of god are you doing? she asked. That's somebody's car.

He laughed and jangled the keys.

Harden him, he said. Whoever he is. Some guy who thinks he's a big deal.

You just did that to some total stranger's car!

I could have put a brick through the windscreen. Chill out about it, Linda!

Linda resolved that she would put an end to things. There would be no next time with Ritchie. But then the next thirteen years became a series of next times, a procession of jobs lost, loans not paid, cars crashed. And all the time that Kit Kat attitude. A week into another job that he could do standing on his head, Ritchie said that the boss gave him a hard time for eating a Twix when he was at his desk. You don't eat until the break, he warned. I wasn't eating a Twix, said Ritchie. The boss said, well I saw you. No, you didn't, Ritchie said, you need to get your facts straight. You didn't see me eating a Twix. You saw me eating a Kit Kat.

The last time Linda saw Ritchie, she brought him three bags of shopping, which included a couple of packets of Kit Kats. It was back when she knew where he was, when he was still in the flat he had moved into, the one that overlooked the football pitch. The smell of churned-up mud always seemed to hang in the air even when the ground was frozen solid. When he answered the door, she saw he had the dregs of a black eye.

What happened you? Linda asked.

Oh, he shrugged. Don't remember. Could have been one of several things.

The place was empty and immaculate. Even in its smallness though there were so many places to sit: a three-piece suite and chairs round the kitchen table, a stool in the hall. Who was ever going to be there for all the chairs? Ritchie was looking so skinny, his shoulders sharp under his jumper. By the kettle there were two empty bottles of some spirit with an Eastern European label and another one half full.

You not working at the moment? she said.

Just looking around at present. Seeing how things lie.

You've got thin, Linda said.

He asked how Danny was.

He's fine. The big eighteen coming up. Can you believe it, Ritchie?

I sure cannot, he said.

Well, yeah. You not going to make me a cup of tea, then?

He didn't have any teabags. The fridge had nothing in it but a bottle of lemonade.

Maybe come round, you know, when it's his birthday, Linda said.

Could do, he said. If he wants me round. But I was

thinking of getting away for a bit. Maybe got an offer of work. Wales. Maybe.

When Linda left, instead of driving home she took a detour to a shop where she bought stuff she thought he would use, Kit Kats included. When he opened the door again to the surprise of seeing her standing there a second time, she said, Here's a few things to keep you going. She had practised saying it as she walked towards the flat so it sounded quite matter of fact and cheerful.

Linda, he said.

Linda didn't contact Rae during the week to ask her how it had gone. She nearly hoped that something bad had happened so that she could be proved right about needing to be worried. I did tell her, she could say to the cops charged with solving the crime, it wasn't that she had no awareness of the risks.

But when Linda went around the next Friday Rae answered the ring of the bell. She was still in the land of the living. She said that it had gone well. Mike was a good laugh and had a lot of interesting stories to tell. A couple of weeks later, Rae told Linda that she was going to go on holiday with him.

A holiday? Where to?

Mexico, Rae said. One of those reservations with everything on site. It's one of those last-minute deals. We thought, know what, let's just go for it.

Linda tried not to sound surprised. Holidays in Mexico, she said. So that's where it's at these days.

The delivery is taking a long time tonight, Rae said.

Maybe I should give them a call.

Up to you, Linda said.

The hotel's called Secrets Bonita Beach Krystal Cancun, Rae said.

What a mouthful.

I doubt we'll be saying it more than once or twice, Linda. Once you're there, you're there. They've got a Wellness Centre and a Scuba Centre. There's tennis courts and mini-golf. And wait until you hear this. If you are in the pool there's waiters who bring round snacks in kayaks.

Trying to envisage that, Linda said. I'm seeing half eaten cocktail sausages bobbing about down the deep end.

Wouldn't have thought so in a classy place like that.

What's it called again?

Secrets Bonita Beach Krystal Cancun.

Still no sign of that takeaway, Linda said. Maybe do give them a ring.

Ritchie was never on time for anything. An arrangement involving any specifics was an opportunity for him not to do what was expected of him. I'm not taking a telling from anyone! was his attitude. Tell him to come at three and he would be there at half past, tell him to come at half past and he would be there at four. There were Sundays when he never turned up for Danny at all. Linda would see Danny leaping up from the sofa and going to the window every time a car went past. One time Danny waited hours for his dad in a burger place in town but Ritchie never turned up.

When Linda phoned he said he was just about to ring her.

You won't believe what happened, he said.

How right you are. I won't believe it.

But wait till you hear.

I'm hearing nothing other than what a selfish person you are.

He said nothing.

Yep. Self-centred. Things happened, okay, I understand that, I accept that.

Linda, shut up, he said.

No, I won't shut up. Why don't you get to fuck asking me to shut up? Let me say something to you. I want you to hear what I'm saying. Don't know what went on, it wasn't your fault, but it wasn't my fault or Danny's fault either. We weren't there. Do you hear, Ritchie? Ritchie?

There was no reply and Linda thought he had left the phone sitting somewhere because she could hear the sound of the radio.

Ritchie.

Just the sound of the radio.

Oh well, there you go. Says it all.

When Linda got home she looked up the hotel that Rae had talked about, Secrets Bonita Beach Krystal Cancun. The water on the website was a saturated, ridiculous blue, the same colour as the saturated, ridiculous sky. She worked out roughly how much it was going to cost them, even allowing for the last-minute deal. Well over a thousand pounds for ten days. She checked the weather forecast for the time when they were going. Consistently lovely. The swimming pools—there were many—were all sweeping curves. There were photos of the Wellness Centre and a dance studio that Rae hadn't mentioned. And such a range of restaurants: a trattoria, a taqueria, a French place with awnings, and an American diner. Breakfast was served by the pool. Linda was able to click on the menus to decide what she might want to have, if she was there. It said the drinks were unlimited, international and domestic, top-shelf spirits. Rae and Mike weren't going to be downing any local hooch. There was a bar called the Winery and it had rows and rows of barrels stacked to the ceiling. The sand was bleached white and the rooms all had telescopes on tripods. She saw it all in the pictures. What would you gaze out at through the telescope? There was just an expanse of blue.

Linda had once visited the place where Ritchie had been sent. It was over on the other side of town. During Ritchie's short-lived career as a taxi driver some guy had asked to be taken there and en route, Ritchie had suddenly decided no, he couldn't take him any further and so he dumped his bags out on the road. The man phoned up to complain. And Ritchie lost his job. The road curved elegantly and the houses, once grand residences, were sub-divided now for offices and businesses. Linda didn't go any closer than the end of the driveway. She stood peering at the place beside the signs for a graphic design studio and a software solutions place. That guy jettisoned at the side of the road was probably into software solutions. She saw the ramp for people with disabilities and that the windows had been recently double glazed and looked particularly plastic. There was staining down the gable wall where water seemed to be leaking from a gutter. All in all, it was an unremarkable and banal place.

Looking at the website and hearing Rae talk had got Linda thinking about how there was no reason why she couldn't go somewhere herself. She could get a cottage somewhere, or go to a spa hotel. She could stay in Dublin, Glasgow, London. It might be that Paris wasn't out of the question, or maybe even Barcelona. But when she looked at prices and availability, it seemed better to stay closer to home.

For some reason, her mind turned to Portrush on the north Antrim coast. It didn't take long to find a bed and breakfast place, Craster House, that looked like it would do her for a few nights. If Rae asked, Linda could say that yes, in fact she was away too. Headed up to Portrush. By yourself? Rae might query. Well, she could keep it vague, oh well, just someone, nothing too serious—if Rae actually asked.

Linda finished work early on the Friday afternoon and, listening to the Beach Boys on the way, drove the fifty miles to Portrush. Again the takeaway wouldn't get their order; she wondered if they even noticed. Did they say, oh we haven't heard from those two this evening? Maybe they had names for her and Rae, Neatso and the Boss and Mr Hot, the way they had for them. Secrets Bonita Beach Krystal Cancun. Maybe at this very minute they were in the Wellness Centre having some kind of treatment. Maybe they were chilling in the relaxation room.

Ritchie used to talk about a rec room. He said about how they were all sitting watching TV one time, one of those nature shows, because that was all that was on. Ritchie said that this young boy who had just arrived was sitting down at the front on the floor and when this plant burst into bloom with the time lapse and all that, well fair enough it was quite sudden and trippy, this wee guy just turned round and his face was full of wonder at it. He looked round expecting them to be amazed too. At a plant. For fuck's sake. My heart sank, Ritchie said. I thought you poor bastard. You stupid bastard.

Craster House overlooked the south strand. It was painted pale pink, like a dessert. There was no one in reception, although there was an envelope on the desk with Lindy written on it in capitals. Lindy sounded fun. Although Linda was also fun, certain Lindas anyway like Linda Lusardi or Linda Lovelace. Inside there were two keys on a fob bearing a picture of the Eiffel Tower and the number eight. Linda, trying to find the room, walked down the corridor and up a flight of stairs, passing on the way three young guys in grey tracksuits who were standing on the landing. One started making noises like a chicken. At that one of the doors opened and two little girls ran out into the corridor then a woman shouted at them in another language and the little girls shot back in, laughing. Craster House didn't feel like a usual hotel but the room was clean and bright. There was an unbroken sea view and an old wicker chair where she could sit to view it.

But Linda didn't want to stay in the room. Once she had left her bag there, she headed out, passing again the young men in the hall who were sitting on the floor. There was still no one in reception. The door had been left open so the wind had blown the brochures for bus tours and attractions all over the floor. Linda picked them up and set them on the desk, closed the door behind her.

The sea in front of her churned grey and black. A couple of surfers lay on their boards as they tried to paddle out into the deep. There was an ice-cream van in the car park she passed and because it was the seaside and she was on holiday, sort of, she got a small cone. When she headed round to the front, she saw that there was already a queue gathering at the big restaurant on the corner. She walked towards the turreted town hall that was opposite the big amusement arcade. It looked different from the last time that she had been there: more concrete, more stone.

The place outside where she and Ritchie had sat watching Danny on a roundabout of cartoon characters wasn't there anymore. The roundabout had flashing lights and made squawking sounds as it moved. Danny waved from the hyper-coloured fish he was sitting on every time he came round.

Ritchie said that they'd once been taken on a trip to Portrush when he was in the place, a rare day out. They'd messed about in the amusements and got chucked out. They'd got out of the carriage in the ghost train and then they'd done something to a gun in the shooting range. Broken it.

And then we were sitting just over there, he said, about six of us and they weren't picking us up for hours and we didn't have any money and the next thing Ian appeared and he had money and we said where did you get that from? He was at the toilet, somebody said. We looked over to where the toilets were and there was a fella coming out, big overcoat. Smart looking. We looked at Ian and then at the guy in the overcoat. Ian says, well if I am having to do it, might as well get paid for doing it. And then Ian used the money to get fish and chips for everybody. Mine went cold really quick and I put them in the bin.

As he told this Danny came round again and again on the roundabout. Linda waved and Ritchie waved. When the roundabout finished, Linda didn't want to get up from the bench where they had been sitting but Ritchie was already on his feet and lifting Danny off. The next stop was the mini car rally.

When Linda went into the amusement place she saw that the ghost train was still there. A straggly little queue waited to be not very scared. She put her money in the machine to get a metal cascade of tokens and then she tried a couple of the Penny Falls machines, losing and winning and losing again. There were bells ringing, electronic squelches from the machines, disco music echoing in the big hall. She thought of Mike and Rae in the Wellness Centre at the Secrets Bonita Beach Krystal Cancun.

Linda needed to get rid of some of the tokens. She didn't want to ask for a refund on them. There was always the log river. She walked along the wet metal to take a seat in the plastic log. The blue of the water was intense. As the mechanism engaged she rose up as the water poured down the gradient. And then the log paused at the top. It wasn't a panoramic view but it was still a moment. She could see the moss that had gathered on the rooftops.

There was a mediocre splash when it moved on again.

On her way back to the hotel, Linda stopped at a mini-market where she bought a bag of sweets and a tortilla wrap. That would keep her going until she decided what she wanted to do later on. She didn't fancy the idea of being somewhere heavy on the high-chairs, where families were sharing giant pizzas or worse, some candle-lit joint full of doe-eyed couples. At Craster House, one of the young men was standing outside. When she pushed the door, she realised it was locked.

That's why I'm standing here, the young guy said. Can't get in.

You rung the bell? Linda asked.

Aye.

Linda rang it. But nobody came.

Fella's not there, the young guy said. So Linda took the keys from her bag and let them both in.

Missus, he said, you don't happen to have any cigarettes? He was eighteen or so, twenty at the most. She could see an inch of his underpants above his track suit bottoms. He tugged at his sleeve, twisted his neck.

No, sorry, I don't smoke, Linda said. And she went back to her room.

She made herself a cup of tea using the old kettle that was in the room and some water from the bathroom tap. She lay back on the bed and watched the television for a while eating the wrap. Had Rae ended up having sex a lot with Mike? She imagined them on the hotel bed with its Egyptian cotton and wonderful mattress. The hotel had a bespoke pillow service so that if you didn't like the one you were given you could request another from a menu. Maybe they had sex all day long and then headed down to the place with the wine barrels for a drink.

She ignored the knock at the door. Nobody knew she was there. It was probably those little kids she saw earlier, the little girls, messing around. But it continued. When she opened the door it was the young guy in the tracksuit.

Hi ya, hello there, he said. Not trying to be funny or anything but would it be okay if I came in for a minute?

Well, not really, Linda said. I'm just—needing to get on with things.

I can't get into my room, that's all.

And then he was there sitting on the bed. There was a metallic taste in Linda's mouth that she knew was fear but she made him a cup of tea in the mug she had used herself. He saw the bag of sweets.

Here can I have a couple of those there? asked.

He said his name was Cathal.

You on holiday here then, Cathal? she asked him.

He laughed. No fucking way. He laughed again. No, I'm not here on a holiday.

What you up to here then?

I'm up to nothing, he said, But I'll be moving on before too long. I got a mate. I'm going to be staying with him next week. This place is a dump. Innit though?

It's not the best really, Linda replied.

We got moved here because the other place was full. Full of old guys. It had dead hot showers though.

He looked at her. Have you been moved here too?

No, she said.

Can I stay with you? he asked. The other ones have moved on. I've got nowhere to go until next Monday. You don't need to be frightened or anything cos I'm not a rapist. I hate rapists. Scum of the earth.

But you've stolen my purse, she said. She could see it tucked into his waistband and only half covered by his T-shirt. He must have taken it when she was making the tea.

Sorry, he said. Shouldn't have done that. Fair dos, here's it back. I got no money though. Haven't really eaten anything in a couple of days. And I have actually been chucked out of this place. Can I stay here?

Why can't you go back to where you're from?

Where's that? he said. Where's that then? His little finger was touching gently an old cold sore at the side of this mouth.

He sighed. He started as if he was going to tell her something.

Fuck it. Can I stay here or can I not?

Her double bed at home had a blue and white striped duvet, and a bedside table at each side. On each of the tables there was a little light. She always put the electric blanket on because she hated getting into a cold bed.

Linda said that she was meant to be there for two nights. But she had changed her mind and she was going to go home. He could stay there if he wanted. He could stay in her place.

But we could maybe go and get something to eat before you go? What do you reckon?

His eyes were a very pale green. A muscle twitched in his jaw.

Get something to eat, have a chat, you know.

He was aware of her looking at him and he put his head down.

What was the harm in going for something to eat, a pizza maybe? She had passed a place earlier on, its candles lit, its tables ready. What was the harm?

No, she said. I need to go. I think I'll just head back this evening. You can stay here, and here's—she rooted in her purse—here's a tenner for you to get something to eat. That enough for you?

He looked at the tenner and put it in his pocket. Thanks, he said in a small voice.

Linda went round to Rae's the next Friday. She was looking tanned but otherwise the same. Rae said she hadn't bought her a present because there really wasn't anything that she could buy that would have suited. It wasn't that kind of a place, she said. You know, they didn't really go in for knick-knacks.

I'm sure the hotel was lovely, Linda said.

It was, no doubt about it. So many different restaurants that you could go to. We ended up a lot in the bar, this lovely one with barrels all stacked up to the roof.

Great.

And we were able to have foods from all over the place.

Cool.

Yeah, it was fine and all that, Rae said. But to be honest I was bored after the first couple of days. See me, I'm active. Couldn't be doing with all that lounging by the pool or going to the chill-out room in the Wellness what have you. Mike loved all that.

But you got on well?

Oh we got on well. But better as friends. Just the way it goes. You live and you learn. What's been happening with you then?

Nothing much.

Same old same old?

Look there's the guy with the food, Linda said.

A blue car had pulled up outside and Rae went to the door.

Well, it's not Neatso, I can tell you that for sure, she said when she brought the bags in. Look at how that's folded.

Rae shouted through from the kitchen that it wasn't the work of the Boss but at least it wasn't Olivia either.

When she came through, she placed the tray with the food on the coffee table and lifted off the plates.

I'll tell you though, she said, Mike works in an area where there is a lot of action. Wait till you hear some of the stories. There was this one time where there were six killed in the one car! And he was the first on the scene. What do you think that looked like?